Tempt Me, Cowboy

Tempt Me, Cowboy

A Copper Mountain Rodeo Novella

Megan Crane

Tempt Me, Cowboy
Copyright © 2013 Megan Crane
Tule Publishing First Printing, May 2016

The Tule Publishing Group, LLC

ALL RIGHTS RESERVED

No part of this book may be used or reproduced in any manner whatsoever without written permission except in the case of brief quotations embodied in critical articles and reviews.

This is a work of fiction. Names, characters, places, and incidents are products of the author's imagination or are used fictitiously. Any resemblance to actual events, locales, organizations, or persons, living or dead, is entirely coincidental

ISBN: 978-1-944925-63-5

Chapter One

SHE WAS EXACTLY the kind of trouble he didn't need.

Jasper Flint could see the woman from halfway down the block, like a shot of bright color against the weathered old brick of his newest acquisition. She hadn't been there when he'd left the railway depot earlier that morning for a run around the outskirts of Marietta, Montana, his brand new home. There'd been nothing but the crisp blue dawn, the hint of the coming winter already there in the chill of the late September morning while Copper Mountain stood high above the town, a sleepy blue and purple giant slouching in the distance.

And the quiet. The blessed quiet and more of the same on the wind. A far cry from the noisy, frantic, nonstop life he'd left behind in Dallas.

An hour and a leisurely five miles later, Jasper was more than ready to face a long day of renovations, the current highlight of the best decision he'd ever made: his early retirement at thirty-five. He was ready to lose himself in the simple joy of *making* instead of *taking*, the sheer, hard won happiness in transforming something old into something new. He wasn't ready for whatever trouble this woman had brought with her, the storm of it swirling around her despite the early morning sunlight and the clear fall day, practically casting the whole street in her shadow.

It was there in the way she stood waiting for him, impatient hands on her sweet hips and her chin tilted up—belligerent and scrappy, like she wanted to exchange a few punches right there in the street. It made him smile. He wouldn't mind getting his hands on her, blonde and cute and with legs that could inspire a man to wax a little poetic even in the blandly conservative clothes she wore, and preferably before she opened her mouth and ruined the perfectly decent fantasy he already had going on.

But he knew her type. Prissy and disapproving, spring-loaded way too tight and, unless he misread that downturned mouth of hers and the glare she aimed at him like she already knew him, constitutionally unhappy.

Not—it went without saying—the sort of woman he usually found hanging around, waiting for him to show up. Not enough cleavage, for one thing. And definitely not enough teased hair. He liked his women cheap and obvious and all but flashing neon signs above their heads to shout out their availability.

This woman looked like trouble. Expensive trouble and a whole lot of work. He was in the market for neither.

Jasper slowed to a stroll as he drew near, eyeing her not-nearly-tight-enough pants and definitely-not-slinky-enough top, that thick blonde hair twisted back from her face in a way that shouted *sensible,* with something uncomfortably close to regret. He wondered what it would be like to have a woman like this—her figure concealed by her outfit instead of starkly presented to him like a Vegas buffet—throw herself at him the way the bimbos did so easily. But that was the paradox, of course. The good girls had steered well clear of him even before he'd had money, like he had darkness grafted onto his very bones and they could scent it in the wind.

He'd learned to live with cheap and calculating. He'd even have said he liked it, the predictability and the ease of that kind of woman, the uncomplicated nature of such mercenary transactions, until now.

"Sorry," he said when he was close, letting his Texas roots have their way with his drawl, and surprised to discover he meant it. "You're not really my type."

She blinked, her lips parting slightly, which drew his attention to what might have been the most carnal mouth in the whole of the West. It hit him like a hammer, pounding an impossible lust through his body to pool in his sex.

What the hell?

"I—what?"

It was like she could read his mind, and it made her stammer.

"I like easy and sleazy." He grinned slightly, imagining

that mouth of hers engaged in practices that would fall under both headings. "I'm afraid I'm true to my redneck roots." He flipped the bottom of his ratty green Stars t-shirt up to wipe at his face, and when he lowered it, was more delighted than he should have been to find her staring at his abdomen with a look on her face that suggested he'd smacked her over the head with a hammer of his own. His grin widened. "I don't really go for the disapproving schoolmarm thing. But I sure do appreciate the thought."

She blinked again. Then understanding flooded over her surprisingly readable face and Jasper watched in fascination as she went pale, then a deep red. A blush? When was the last time he'd seen a woman blush? His ex-wife had been incapable of it—and, for that matter, just about everything else it turned out a marriage required.

Jasper banished thoughts of *that* blessedly short-lived disaster, and concentrated on the woman in front of him instead. He couldn't seem to keep himself from imagining what that blush might look like in far more interesting places. And were those *freckles* across her delicate cheeks, complicating the creamy sweep of her skin?

He didn't understand why he found that so intriguing. Or why it made him *want* in a way he hadn't felt in so long, it took him a moment or two to recognize what that particular feeling, sharp and intense and roaring in him so loudly, even was.

"It's seven thirty in the morning." She sounded scandalized. Her eyes were a blue to rival the Montana sky, and they widened in what had to be horror, which he felt like a heat wave throughout his body, reminding him how dark and perverse he was compared to an undoubtedly pure, small town sweetheart like this one. "On a *Monday*."

"It wouldn't matter if it was the sweet spot of a Saturday night," he told her, enjoying himself immensely despite his own twisted soul. It wasn't like he could do anything about it, could he? "It still wouldn't work out, unless you're hiding a honky tonk or two beneath that Head of the PTA outfit of yours."

"I most certainly am not." But her hands moved to the ruffled part of her blouse, then her quiet little belt buckle, as if she'd forgotten what she was wearing and had to remind herself by touch. Or make sure it was still there.

Or maybe she was as baffled by these garments, neither of which he'd ever seen on a woman under sixty-five years of age, as he was.

"I'm afraid we're just not meant to be, darlin'," he drawled, more Texas in his voice than usual and a fire he couldn't quite control beneath it.

That rattled her for a moment, he could see it in that intense blue of her eyes, but then she squared her shoulders and tilted that chin of hers back up anyway. *Scrappy,* he thought again, and with a purely male jolt of approval that boded ill for the both of them, he just knew it.

"What on earth would make you think someone would

show up and proposition you at this hour?" she demanded. "What kind of degenerate are you?"

Jasper realized then that she had no idea who he was. He found that notion wildly liberating. And, strangely, arousing. He couldn't remember the last time someone hadn't known who he was and acted accordingly. He'd forgotten what it was like—the honest responses that had nothing to do with his net worth, the total lack of artifice or calculation, that look on her face that suggested he was nothing but a man, and a rather unappetizing one at that.

He thought he loved this place already, and he'd been here all of two days.

"The kind of degenerate you appear to be hanging around on the street waiting for," he replied easily, not at all surprised that he was enjoying himself now. His brows arched up. "At seven-thirty. On a *Monday*."

THIS WAS MUCH worse than Chelsea had imagined.

I heard it from Carol Bingley myself, Mama had said on Saturday, standing in the doorway to the kitchen, her entire small frame radiating tension and fury, which usually made everyone in a six mile radius duck for cover and/or hide.

Everyone except Chelsea, that was, because it was Chelsea's duty to take care of her. Margot was down in Salt Lake City tending to her ever-expanding family, Nicky had stayed in North Carolina after college and married a woman who had no intention of leaving the area, and Daddy had died almost fifteen years ago now, which left Mama to Chelsea.

Whether she liked it or not. Mostly, of course, she liked it fine. Mostly.

Sometimes I think Carol Bingley makes things up just to feel important, Chelsea had replied in a light tone, pretending to be deeply involved in the preparation of her sandwich, not that she could imagine eating anything with Mama glaring at her like that, so accusingly, like Chelsea had betrayed her in some way. *It has to feel like a pretty small life, spending all day in a pharmacy when you're not even a pharmacist, snooping on people every time they drop off a prescription or pick up an extra tube of toothpaste—*

The depot has been sold. Mama had intoned it like a death knell, and it rang through the kitchen like one, then inside of Chelsea, because she knew what it meant. That she'd failed. That she'd let Mama down. That she was as useless as Mama had always told her she was, though she tried very hard not to let that get to her. *The new owner—some Texan roughneck—is moving in this weekend. Congratulations, Chelsea. That Wright girl*—she meant Chelsea's best friend Jenny, of whom Mama had never approved, and it pained Chelsea deeply that it was because of where Jenny had lived growing up—*is bettering herself by marrying* a Monmouth *while the Crawford family legacy is lost forever. What do you have to say to that?*

Don't worry, Mama, she'd said. Rashly, perhaps, and it

wasn't like her mother listened anyway. Not to her. *I'll fix it. I promise.*

Even if she didn't want to fix it. Even if she secretly thought that Mama was the broken thing, and worried that she was, too, by association.

Even if she wasn't entirely sure that marrying *a Monmouth* was the best thing for her best friend, not that she'd shared that unsolicited opinion with Jenny or anyone else, which meant she wasn't so sure being *a Crawford* meant much, either.

She shivered now, though the fall morning wasn't particularly cold, and focused her energy on the strange man before her.

He didn't look like a roughneck—not that Chelsea had the slightest idea what a roughneck was supposed to look like, only that Mama thought such people were far, far beneath her. Even further beneath her than everybody else, that was.

This man was long and lean, and built out of the kind of smooth muscles that spoke of long hours of hard, manual labor instead of weight machines in the gym. He was wearing a t-shirt with too many holes and a pair of track pants, and wasn't even breathing heavily, though the t-shirt showed that he'd worked out hard. He had too-long dark hair with hints of gold that spoke of the Texas sun she'd heard in his voice, and that looked as if he'd scraped it back from his face with his fingers. He hadn't shaved. Possibly not in days, though that rasp of stubble wasn't yet a beard. It made him look… disconcertingly untamed, and this was Montana, home of untamed things of all kinds.

And the way he looked at her, with that little crook to his mouth and that gleam in his hazel eyes she wasn't sure she wanted to identify, made her heart turn achy little somersaults in her chest.

Or maybe that was a panic attack. It wouldn't be her first.

"I'm Chelsea Collier," she said stiffly, not sure what was happening to her.

He was tall in a way that made her feel tiny and delicate, despite the fact she was wearing her dizzyingly high three inch heels—the ones with the platform bottoms she'd picked up in Bozeman with Jenny while trying on her Maid of Honor's dress for Jenny's wedding the following week—and hadn't been the slightest bit *delicate* in her whole life. It occurred to her that she hadn't had to introduce herself to someone new in quite a long while, and that made her feel oddly vulnerable, too.

"Chelsea *Crawford* Collier," she amended.

He laughed. It was a gruff, male sound, that worked over her skin and down beneath it, winding around and around the center of her and pulling taut.

"That's a whole lot of Cs for one woman," he said, that laughter still rich in his voice, making her feel shivery for no good reason at all. "What were your parents thinking? What was wrong with every other letter in the alphabet?"

Chelsea summoned her best frown, the one she'd perfected in her years containing boisterous history students at the high school. What was one disreputable-looking man next to packs of unruly teenagers?

"You're new here, so perhaps you don't know that the Crawford family was one of Marietta's First Families," she said reprovingly, aware that she sounded uncomfortably like her mother. That snooty intonation, even the way she was looking at him, as if the name *Crawford* was branded into the side of Copper Mountain standing in the distance. Was this what she had to look forward to? Slowly becoming Mama? But she couldn't seem to stop herself, and the sad truth was that she knew the answer to that already. "Barton Dudley Crawford, my ancestor and one of Montana's great visionaries, brought the railway here in 18—"

"This railway?" he nodded toward the old railway line that ran behind the depot building, and unlike her history students, didn't look even slightly cowed when she scowled at him for interrupting her. "My railway?"

She didn't like his possessiveness, which was another sign she was becoming Mama much faster than she was comfortable with, so she opted to ignore it.

"The very same," she replied primly. "The Marietta Railway Depot is a symbol of our town's rich copper rush past, and stands as a monument to Barton Crawford as well as the many contributions of the Crawford family to this town and to this region since."

A little speech that she was fairly certain she'd heard Mama deliver to the postman only last week, as she was wont to do. *You are turning into her even as you speak,* that dire voice inside of her warned. *It's already happening.*

"Is this what people do for fun around here? Accost newcomers on the sidewalk to give them unsolicited history lessons?" He laughed again, and again, the sound of it did things to her she didn't understand. Or like. "This is definitely not Dallas."

"I'm trying to tell you that you need to make the depot into a museum," she snapped, and even though her little-used temper was flaring, she still caught the way the man before her stilled. He was dangerous, she realized in a sudden flash of insight. Far more dangerous than that easy smile of his let on. "That's what it's supposed to be. What's it's meant to be. I've spent the last year fundraising. The rodeo will be here in two weeks and we're going to have the final push—"

"I'll stop you right there," he said, interrupting again, and she didn't know why that look in his eyes was so unnerving. Like he could see straight through her, to all those shadowy places where she was never Crawford enough, not for Mama.

You're a Collier all the way through, Mama had sniffed whenever Chelsea did something she didn't like—which was more often these days, now that Chelsea's relationship with Tod Styles was over and she was "without prospects." Mama preferred prospects. *Collier straight down to the bone, and nary a speck of Crawford blood to be seen.*

Margot and Nicky, of course, were 100% percent Crawford while they stayed away, though that percentage seemed to dip considerably whenever they visited. Which was probably why they did it so seldom.

There were times, Chelsea reflected, when she found all of this—even Mama's high opinion of herself—funny. Endearing. But today didn't seem to be one of those times.

"I'm Jasper Flint," he said, and then paused, almost as if he expected a reaction to that—but then laughed when Chelsea only continued to scowl at him. "Of course," he said, shaking his head. "You must be the only woman I've met in the past ten years who doesn't have the slightest idea who I am."

"Why would I know who you are?" Chelsea demanded, but even as she did, she realized she should have paid more attention to Mama's very long, very acerbic diatribe about him this weekend. Saturday *and* Sunday, and so what if Chelsea was trying to grade papers? The trouble was, the only way Chelsea knew how to manage her mother was to very actively *not* pay attention to the specifics of the things she said, but to let it all wash over her like the weather. It was a survival tactic she'd perfected a long, long time ago.

But she had the sinking feeling that Carol Bingley knew exactly who this man was. Which meant her mother did, too, and had no doubt shared it all with her while she was only pretending to listen. Which meant she should probably have looked into that before showing up on his doorstep this morning on her way to school, all fired up to do… something.

Jasper Flint only shook his head at her again, an unholy amusement moving over his lean, intriguing face, as if she was deeply entertaining.

No one had ever looked at her like that in her life, and Chelsea felt her breath leave her body as something blisteringly hot moved over her, through her. Confusing her and intriguing her at once.

"I can't say that I care too much about the history of this town, or of your family," he said, in an amiable tone at complete odds with his words. "Mind you, I can barely stand the sight of my own family, so you shouldn't feel too insulted." There was some current there, lurking beneath the seemingly light words, almost a shadow behind his curiously bright gaze, but Chelsea couldn't name it. "And I'm not particularly interested in museums. I like beer, so I'm building a microbrewery. You can come by when it's open and have one." His lips twitched. "On me."

"A microbrewery?" Chelsea knew she sounded aghast, as if the very idea of beer made her want to swoon, like the prudish schoolmarm he'd already accused her of being—but that was only because she could anticipate her mother's reaction to this news. It might blow off the top of Copper Mountain. "But the depot is a landmark! A piece of Marietta's history!"

"Which I'm guessing your hoity-toity First Family couldn't afford to buy, much less repair, or we wouldn't be having this conversation."

He still had all that Texas in his voice, but somehow, that drawl went cool. And it tore her up, though she didn't know why.

"When did you buy it?" she asked.

"About two months ago." His hazel gaze narrowed, as if he was turning that question over in his head. "Does that matter?"

"Not to you, I'd imagine."

But it meant a great deal to her. It meant she'd been lied to, repeatedly, *again*—but she couldn't do anything about that now. Here.

"I don't have much use for monuments, Triple C," Jasper said quietly. "I don't like history lessons and I don't care for preaching." His eyes remained curiously intent on hers. "I think this is the prettiest spot in Montana, which is why I'm here. And as I said, I like beer. I don't see this conversation getting any more productive than that, do you?"

Chelsea fought to keep her panic under control. To say nothing of her temper.

"What can I do to convince you of the error of your ways?" she asked, desperately. "You only just moved here. Maybe if I take you on a tour, if I show you why this is all so important, you'll change your mind."

"I won't."

"How do you know?"

"It's my mind, Triple C. I'm pretty well-acquainted with it."

"An inflexible mind is a sign of weakness. Weakness and fear."

"Do you think reverse psychology is going to work?" But he was smiling. "You have an interesting approach to the sales pitch. And I won't lie, I think it's cute."

"There has to be something I can do," she blurted out, too panicked to register the fact he'd called her *cute*. "To at least make you *listen*."

She watched his marvelous eyes light up then, with a fire that sang in her in ways that made her feel weak, like she'd forgotten to eat for a week. His head tilted to one side as he regarded her, and Chelsea had never felt anything like it before. That slow perusal, that terrible intensity in his hazel gaze, that small crook to his lips that hit her like a punch in the belly. She felt stripped naked right there on the street, where anyone could see and, judging from the number of cars that had gone by throughout this conversation, quite a few people had seen and were no doubt *even now* reporting back to her mother that she was consorting with the enemy.

"Come back here dressed like a woman your actual age," he suggested. "You look like you're trying to pretend you're at least sixty-five. My guess? You're thirty. Maybe."

She frowned down at herself, then at him.

"I'm a schoolteacher. This is a perfectly appropriate outfit."

"Let me guess. History?"

She didn't know why his amusement pricked at her. "As a matter of fact, yes."

"Is it dress like an octogenarian day? I suspect you'll win first prize."

"You don't have to play games with me," she said, furious, and something else unfamiliar that she was afraid to look at too closely. "Or does it amuse you to insult complete strangers within five minutes of meeting them?"

"Only the pretty ones," he said, looking wholly unrepentant. "Come back in a pair of jeans that show off that ass and I promise I'll listen to you. If that's what you want."

He nodded in some parody of good manners, then, as if he hadn't said something *heinous,* the kind of thing that absolutely nobody said to someone like her. Ever.

And Chelsea stood there, stunned, and watched Jasper Flint saunter away like the glorious male animal he was, confident and lazy and totally unbothered by what had happened between them. What he'd said.

Into the depot building which should never have been his.

Which she was going to have to find a way to reclaim, despite him.

Chapter Two

"YOU LIED TO me," Chelsea said in as measured a tone as she could manage.

Which possibly wasn't very *measured* at all, she could admit to herself.

"Lied is a pretty strong word, Chels," Tod Styles replied, all bluster and those bright red spots in his cute, boyish cheeks, which, she knew perfectly well, meant he was lying through his teeth.

She'd discovered that the hard way, when she'd accused him of cheating on her during their ill-advised eighteen months of dating and he'd vociferously denied it, every time.

Including that last time, when she'd walked in to find him *in the act*. His cheeks had been red that night, too. Like twin flags of dishonesty painted right there on his face.

"Please don't call me that," Chelsea said, trying to stay cool. Calm. Trying to remind herself that Tod was actually a perfectly nice man, except if you happened to date him.

Nothing at all like the woman who had screamed bloody murder when she'd seen him thrashing around on top of

Leona Markham on his back deck on July 4th. As if he'd stabbed her in the heart when the truth was, she'd never loved him as much as she thought she should have. *Calm down, Chels,* was what he'd said them in the same tone he'd just used now. Still naked, like her *reaction* to what he was doing was the problem.

She tried to force herself back into the present, where he was thankfully clothed.

"You sold the depot right out from under me. Secretly. You knew what I was trying to do and you sold it anyway, then let me carry on making preparations for the rodeo fundraiser. Were you ever going to tell me, Tod? Or were you planning to let me go ahead and make a fool of myself?"

She couldn't possibly be the only one with déjà vu, could she?

Tod leaned back in his chair, which creaked loudly, reminding Chelsea that they weren't alone in the realty office he ran with his mother, the fearsome Elinor, who had told Chelsea in the first week of her relationship that her son was regrettably just like his father: all boy, no man. Chelsea wished she'd listened. Elinor wasn't in the office today, but Chelsea didn't have to turn around to know that their secretary, Alisa, would be all pricked ears and flying thumbs, texting every word of this interaction to half of Marietta before it was done. In Alisa's ear and out like a megaphone, she knew, but at least there was no malice in it. That was how it went.

Sometimes she wished she'd taken her siblings' lead and moved far, far away, to a place where no one knew her, or her family, or every last scandalous detail of her terrible relationship with Tod, including that she'd foolishly believed it would lead to marriage.

It was that last part that she found the most humiliating now.

"Can I be blunt?" Tod asked, and she could see that he was trying to be kind, which only made the humiliation rage higher.

I'm just not the monogamous type, he'd told her on the front lawn of his house that last, embarrassing night, still buttoning up his khakis, his cheeks no longer quite so bright and his light brown hair messy. *Not yet, anyway. That's for the kind of girl I want to* marry, *Chels.*

Remembering their unfortunate dating history wasn't helping anything, Chelsea thought then. She stood in front of Tod's desk, her arms crossed in front of her, ignoring the fact her feet felt swollen from a day spent standing in front of classrooms in her ridiculous shoes. Ignoring how much she'd like to use one of those wickedly high heels to slap that look from his face—if, of course, she was the sort who believed in violence. Which she was not.

"I've never known how to stop you," she replied. If Tod registered the dryness in her tone, he didn't react to it.

"Flint paid in cash. The full asking price. And let's face it, you were never going to raise the money for the down payment." He shrugged. "It was business, Chelsea. Pure and simple."

"It's very convenient that your business happened to undermine me, isn't it?" she asked, not sure if she was angry or sad, and wishing she could rewind everything and never take him up on that initial invitation to dinner. "Or was that just a bonus?"

"I'm sorry if I led you on, Chelsea," Tod said now, making her feel homicidal and deeply humiliated all at once, which was pretty much how she'd been feeling about the whole thing since that night in July. "I should have made it clear from the start that I wasn't that interested. I feel bad that your feelings got so involved."

That was the worst part, she knew, staring at him. Her feelings hadn't been involved, not that anyone would believe her if she said so. She'd thought Tod was her chance. The answer to her prayers. Her way to stay in Marietta, the place she loved so much, without having to stay forever in that drafty old house on the hill with Mama. Her way to have the things she'd always wanted—her own house, her own man, her own family—without having to turn her back on her responsibilities and in so doing, turn into someone she didn't want to become. Tod was a local boy, his family going back generations in the area, with the kind of deep roots that matched hers.

And besides, her mother had always spoken, if not highly of the Styles family, then at least without the scorn she reserved for some others. It had seemed like such a perfect solution. And she'd always liked Tod well enough. He'd been a few years above her in school, friendly and nice. Liked by almost everybody. A part of the community.

She should have dated her neighbor's Labrador retriever instead. Sparky had all of the same qualities she'd liked in Tod, plus an actual sense of loyalty.

"Thank you, Tod," she said stiffly, when she was sure she could speak without betraying any of her conflicting emotions, or indulging her heretofore unknown lust for violence. "I certainly enjoy as many reminders of our relationship as possible."

"A word of advice, Chels," he said, shaking his head sadly, which was one more patronizing gesture closer to her losing her temper, which seemed a lot closer to snapping today than usual. Someone should probably warn him that he was flirting with disaster, she thought, since he seemed so unaware of it himself. "This obsession with the depot isn't a good idea. You need to let it go before you turn yourself into your mother."

The fact that Tod, of all people, was voicing the worst of her fears, felt like an indignity too far today. She felt it pulse behind her temples like a headache.

"I don't think you know my mother well enough to make that determination," she said frostily. "And I know you don't know me well enough. Or at all."

"You're not doing yourself any favors." He let his gaze

travel from her admittedly raggedy chignon down her neatly buttoned navy and white blouse with the ruffles along the placket to her perfectly serviceable work pants. When Jasper had done the same thing this morning, there'd been heat in it, and amusement. Her whole body had felt like a lantern only he could switch on. Tod's gaze made her feel itchy and annoyed. "You're on a fast track to ending up rattling around that old house for the rest of your life, muttering about the Crawford family's long gone glory days. Just like her."

"I teach history, Tod," she bit out. "I don't have to live it, thank you."

He sighed, like she was the one trying *his* patience.

"I'm sorry about the depot, I really am. But it was never going to happen. And if your mother cared about the town as much as she cared about the Crawford family legacy, she'd understand that what Flint is going to do benefits way more people than some museum ever would. It's going to be gathering place. Families, local bands. A place for the whole community. People want that. They're tired of paying homage to the First Families."

"Spoken like someone who isn't one of the First Families," she replied lightly, loud enough for Alisa to hear and transmit to one and all, something she knew at once she'd regret later, when she was less furious and not so easily goaded. "I always forget how jealous you are."

But after she stormed out of the office with as much dignity as she had left, his words stayed with her as if he'd chased her out into the street himself.

It destroyed any childish satisfaction she might have gotten from getting that last word.

Chelsea stopped for a moment and stood there, letting the fall afternoon seep into her. The sun was still bright and warm, though there was a kick beneath it that whispered summer was already over for another year, and these huge, bright days were nothing but pretty distractions. She remembered running along these sidewalks as a girl, down to the park by the river and then back again. Grey's Saloon hunkered over the corner opposite her, complete with swinging doors on the front and that balustraded balcony running along the second story, where the prostitutes had displayed their wares back when Marietta was little more than an outpost and Grey's—the oldest building in town—was as much a bordello as a saloon.

Mama didn't like the fact that Greys—purveyors of sin going back generations—were actually *more* original Mariettan than the Crawfords. *They make their presence known, don't they?* she always said when forced to acknowledge the existence of the saloon, or even the outdoor adventure outfit one of the other Grey brothers ran from an office above the town's bookstore.

Crawfords aren't flashy, Mama had told them over and over again growing up, despite the fact they lived in one of the area's historic old homes, rich in rambling, Victorian splendor up in the hills above the town. *Crawfords are genteel.*

It had taken Chelsea a long time to understand that what her mother meant was that the Crawfords had once had a great deal more money than anyone else had, and had fancied themselves many social classes above families like the Greys, hence their relocation out of the town proper. And that what they had left now was their heritage. And far too much pride.

Every now and again the weight of that heritage—and what it meant to her mother, and thus to Chelsea because she loved her mother and wanted to make her happy—made Chelsea feel flattened down to the ground beneath it.

But Main Street was like a postcard in the golden light today, a perfect jewel of a western town, and much as she sometimes dreamed of running off and shirking her responsibilities, she knew she wouldn't. She couldn't. She was as much a part of this town as Grey's, her roots almost as deep into the rich Montana soil beneath her feet, and she was a woman who liked to feel connected that way.

She studied the saloon for a moment, considering. She wasn't much for drinking in the afternoon, and she'd never cared much for surly Jason Grey, the current proprietor, no matter how much she'd liked his daughter, Joey, who'd been in her same class back in high school. But Grey's looked particularly inviting today. She frowned at it for a moment, then turned her attention to the mountains, instead. Beautiful Copper Mountain loomed there, brooding and impassive, the way it had her whole life. Watching. Waiting.

For what, she still didn't know.

And the truth was, she was a thirty-year-old woman and she was afraid to go home and face her mother. What did that say about her?

But she knew what it said. Sometimes she thought it was written on her: *Lifelong coward. Afraid. Hiding all her life.*

Chelsea heard the motor first. It was different from the usual motorcycles that ripped through the town, most of them headed to or from Grey's, or further east along the highway toward places like Sturgis. This one sounded... sleeker. It purred like a lion, deep-throated and smooth, and she knew. She knew who it was even before it pulled up beside her, silver and gleaming in the afternoon light, then backed up to the curb at an arrogant angle.

There was absolutely no reason her heart should twist in her chest, then clatter so hard against her ribs.

She'd done a little research on Jasper Flint over her lunch period at school today. Meaning she'd typed his name into Google and saw exactly why he'd been so surprised she hadn't recognized him, or at least his name. And why he'd think it perfectly normal to be propositioned no matter what time of day it was.

Jasper Flint wasn't simply rich. He was quite literally *filthy* rich. He and his brother Jonah had taken their family's small well stimulation company and built it into a major competitor in the oil market, providing hydraulic fracturing services to the oil and gas industry just as the shale boom was blowing up in Texas—before selling it just over a year ago for a rumored four billion.

No wonder he'd bought the depot outright. That was pocket change to a man like him.

She frowned at him as he climbed off his bike, which she didn't have to know a single thing about motorcycles to know was astonishingly rare and expensive. He didn't bother with a helmet, which meant she was treated to an uninterrupted view of Jasper Flint in all his considerable glory. Packed into a pair of jeans and grey t-shirt, with a dark blue hooded sweatshirt on top, he should have looked disreputable and even rumpled.

Instead, he looked more like a god sent down from above to tempt her. Casually perfect, windblown and far too good-looking, from that disheveled hair of his to his scuffed boots, and all that smooth, mouthwatering muscle in between.

He pulled off his sunglasses and smirked at her, and Chelsea had the uneasy notion that he could read every single inappropriate thought she had right there on her face, like it was a billboard.

"I'm guessing from that look on your face that you know who I am," he said, that drawl of his like honey, thick and sweet, confirming her fears.

"Your twin brother is busy buying up ranchland north of Flathead Lake, apparently," she said by way of a reply, afraid that if she looked directly into his hazel eyes she'd go blind, like he was the sun. "Why are you opening microbreweries out here in the middle of nowhere? I'd think your tastes ran more to empire building and the wholesale destruction of natural environments in a cynical bid to line your own pockets."

And then she aimed her best prim schoolteacher smile at him, deliberately. His smirk turned into something more dangerous.

"Look at that. It's like we're old friends."

"I hope you're happy," she said, meaning to maintain her almost believably light tone but losing it somewhere as she spoke. "History is important. Just because you don't have any of your own doesn't mean you should stamp all over other people's."

"I wasn't planning to stamp, necessarily." He eyed her, sending that curious heat stampeding through her again, then jerked his head toward the saloon. "Thought I might walk calmly into Grey's and enjoy a little bit of Marietta history first hand. Feel free to join me." That quirk of his lips shouldn't affect her like that, surely. "We can talk about the many and varied reasons women proposition me, at any time of the day or night."

Chelsea opened her mouth to say no, automatically, because *of course* she wasn't the type of woman who went into bars with strange men in the middle of the afternoon.

But the mountain was behind him, still waiting, and the light was so thick and golden it made him look like he was made of the stuff, like the kind of man sculptors tried to capture in bronze. She didn't have to turn around to know that Tod was likely looking out the window of his office at this interaction, that Alisa was probably texting it to anyone within a hundred miles who wasn't around to witness it, and that Carol Bingley herself was either pressed to her own window down at the pharmacy or letting one of her spies do it for her. Because the good news and the bad news of life in a place like Marietta was that everyone knew everyone else's business.

Mama's phone would be ringing right now, if it hadn't rung already. She'd be peering down toward town from her lofty, disapproving perch high in the foothills, and Chelsea would start paying for this indiscretion the moment she walked in the door. Why not make it worth the bother?

And the truth was, no one else in Marietta looked at her like she was edible and he was very, very hungry.

No one else looked at her much at all—and why should they? She'd been exactly the same since birth. Dependable. Dutiful. The standard bearer for what was left of the once-mighty Crawford family, just as her mother wanted, and some part of her had even enjoyed that. She'd babysat for half the town and tutored for the rest, and they all treated her with the same mix of affably mild interest and polite support. She'd lived at home while she'd taken classes at Montana State over in Bozeman because it was easier and cheaper, and she'd settled into her life right here in Marietta without a hitch, like she might as well be one of the cottonwood trees down by the river, rooted in deep to this place. Immovable.

She'd wanted all of that. She still wanted it.

But you're thirty, not sixty-five, a voice inside of her whispered. *You deserve a few interesting afternoons, don't you?*

The only exciting thing that had ever happened to her had actually been happening between Tod and Leona. She'd only witnessed it, and had been patronized about it every day since.

So because it was the last thing anyone would ever expect her do—because *she* couldn't believe she'd do such a thing and *he* looked like he expected her to make the sign of the cross and run for safety and holy water, Chelsea smiled up at Jasper Flint as if he really was the sun and it was still the height of summer.

"Thank you," she said. "I'd love to join you."

Chapter Three

THAT MISS TRIPLE C was not a regular in Grey's Saloon was obvious by the way she walked inside, gingerly, as if she expected a pack of hellhounds to descend upon her the moment she set foot in the comfortably dim interior.

Jasper's impression was confirmed by the way she looked around wildly, gulped, then strode with more determination than enthusiasm toward the long, wide bar, straight up to the unsmiling older man who stood there, glowering. A glower which turned thunderous as he looked from Chelsea to Jasper and then back again.

"Are you lost?" the man asked, his voice gruff and rude.

"Hello, Mr. Grey," she chirped, because of course Triple C was polite to the scariest son of a bitch bartender Jasper had seen in a while. She was wearing *ruffles,* for God's sake. Ruffles and that perky voice, and why the hell was he hard? Rock hard, like he might die from it.

Unbelievable, he thought, and followed her to the bar.

"Thought I told you to call me Jason a decade back," the man growled, but his ferocious glare was on Jasper now.

"Mr. Grey is my father, and I can't say I'm particularly close with him."

"Your father is a lovely man," Chelsea said staunchly, which made it perfectly clear to Jasper that whatever the man was, he certainly wasn't *lovely*. Jason's snort confirmed it. "My friend and I would like two whiskeys," she continued, and if he wasn't mistaken, that was pure bravado in her voice then, pushing back the perkiness and taking on a hint of huskiness when she looked at him. "Right?"

"I won't decline," he said, all drawl and no bravado, only need.

The look the bartender shot him was about as unfriendly as it was possible to get without involving fists. Jasper grinned, in a manner he knew perfectly well could only be described as *shit-eating*.

"Where's Reese?" Chelsea asked, then turned to Jasper as if she didn't expect the surly older man to answer her, which he didn't. "Reese is like a surrogate member of the Grey family. He helps run this place."

Meaning, he was probably the one Jasper had seen behind the bar when he'd wandered in here on Saturday night after moving his meager belongings into the spacious top floor of the depot, which he'd decided to make a kind of loft. He filed away that information, along with the fact that both men carried themselves like ex-military—always a good thing to keep in mind when dealing with other men on their home territory. He waved away Chelsea's attempt to pay for the drinks, added a beer to the order and a glass of appalling-looking red wine he had the feeling she didn't even want despite asking for it, and then steered her away from the bar and Jason Grey's relentless glower.

She chattered all the way to a booth in the far corner, filling Jasper in on what seemed to be every last member of the Grey family who had ever lived. A cousin in DC. Another in San Francisco. He got the impression of a lot of daughters who cared about as much for their dour father as Jasper did, and a runaway wife. Chelsea either didn't notice the tension emanating from behind the bar, or was valiantly ignoring it.

Or, he thought when they sat down and she was clutching her shot glass like it was a life preserver, this was just nerves.

"I make you nervous," he said.

She frowned. "Of course you don't."

He clearly did, and that, perversely, made him feel as relaxed as if he'd just had a full body massage from someone very curvy and morally questionable. He felt lazy and something far darker, far more intent, as he studied her.

"Is it this bar? Doesn't look like you come in here much."

"For all you know I dance naked on the tables every night of the week," she snapped at him, and he wasn't the only one who noticed how the word *naked* seemed to sit there and spin on the dark wood tabletop between them. She swallowed, hard, like she couldn't think about anything else. He knew he couldn't.

"Every night except the last two, then."

"You spent your first two nights in town at the saloon?"

"You say that like it's a bad thing. I consider it my own, personal welcome wagon. Only without cookies."

There was something about the way strands of her blonde hair kept falling out of that twist of hers that made him… edgy. Hungry, maybe, like he wanted to reach over and pull the whole mess of it down just to see it swirl around her shoulders, thick and bright. It was much too hard to keep himself from it. Much, much harder than it should have been.

"I wouldn't dream of judging you," she said, and then her lips twitched as the tone she'd used—the very definition of *judgmental*—echoed there between them. "Not too openly, anyway."

He raised his shot glass and waited. Her face was so open he almost wanted to shield her from the rest of the bar, who surely didn't deserve to read every last thought she broadcast there. Her alarm, her desire. Her nervousness. Her fascinating resolve. She swallowed hard, then picked up her own shot glass, and he watched her chin rise and her shoulders go back, like she was talking herself into it. Into *this*.

His little pugilist.

"To history," he said.

Her blue eyes narrowed.

"To history," she replied, and then held her shot glass still while he gently tapped his to the side.

Jasper tossed the whiskey back, then had the pleasure of watching her do the same. Her eyes watered, her face reddened, but she only coughed once. Then sat there, frozen, staring back at him as if she'd been slapped.

"Do that a lot, do you?"

He was mocking her, and she obviously knew it. She blinked until her eyes lost that hectic glitter, then glared at him.

"I love nothing more than a shot of whiskey at the end of a long school day, thank you," she retorted.

"Tell me, Triple C," he murmured, leaning in close, feeling daggers in his back from across the room but unable to care about anything but that frankly carnal mouth of hers and the way it parted slightly as he took up too much of the space between them. "Is this your big rebellion? Tossing back shots in the middle of town with a stranger?"

He didn't know what he expected. Her to laugh, maybe. Or to suggest a more satisfying form of rebellion the way his usual sort of woman would. He certainly didn't expect that flash of vulnerability in her gaze, or the way she shifted in her seat, then looked down.

"It sounds so pitiful when you say it."

"Not at all, darlin'," he heard himself say, more drawl than sense. "I'm an excellent way to start a downward spiral. We'll have you table dancing within the week."

He thought he saw the glimmer of a smile in the corner of her mouth.

"I don't think multi-billionaires can claim to be anyone's downward anything," she said, and it took a moment for him to understand why it got under his skin. It was the brisk, matter-of-fact way she said it.

She wasn't flirting with him. She was simply stating the obvious.

It was remarkably refreshing.

"A rich bastard's still a bastard."

She looked up then, her gaze solemn. "That's true. My ancestor Barton Crawford was a very rich man, for his time. And by all accounts, an ass."

"Then by all means, let's make him a museum."

Her smile was faint, but there, and it should have alarmed him that he viewed that like his own, personal triumph. But he was too focused on the way her fingers clasped the stem of her wine glass, more elegant than their surroundings, and too obsessed with imagining what she'd look like out of those fussy clothes she wore. Naked, he thought, and spread out across his bed, nothing but heat in her eyes and a smile on that decadent mouth of hers—

He couldn't remember the last time he'd wanted something like this, so badly and completely. Because he couldn't remember the last time he'd wanted something he couldn't snap his fingers and have, just like that.

"It's my mother," she said. Then stopped and looked

down, as if biting back whatever she'd been about to say. When she met his gaze again, hers was resigned, filled with a sort of amused love he recognized, and that resolve. "Life hasn't been as kind as it could have been to my mother. Her father lost all his money and then my father died in a great deal of his own debt. She had to sell off all her family's land, but kept the old house, because her ancestors built it so long ago it was free. My older sister and brother provided her with grandchildren, but they don't live here, where she would dedicate herself to educating them on what she has left of her legacy. So what she has is family history." She shrugged. "As obsessions go, hers is mild."

But what Jasper saw were all the things she didn't say, stuck in between the lines. It was all there on her open, expressive face, not at all hidden by that hint of wariness in her too-blue eyes. He couldn't remember the last time he'd wanted to reach out and touch another person like this, like it was a physical necessity.

He fought it off.

"Doesn't sound like there's much room for you in there."

"This is Big Sky country. There's always room." But her chin was up, and he doubted it. "I love teaching and I'm good at it. I've lived here all my life and wouldn't leave if I could. We have a lot going on, though maybe not by your Dallas standards." She sat too straight, too still. "There's what will probably be the wedding of the year next Saturday, big and brash and beautiful. Then the rodeo a week after that, and we'll go all out for both. The wedding is one of our own and the rodeo is tradition."

"I never said I didn't like tradition."

"You don't have to say it." She looked him up and down. "You *are* it." She lifted up her glass then set it down again. "You're not going to stay here. You know you're not. You have a whole world to play in, and what's one small town next to that? You'll make your microbrewery and then you'll get bored with it, so you'll hire someone else to run it or you'll sell it."

There wasn't a shred of accusation in her tone, not a hint of it in her gaze, and yet he stiffened.

"No point in living the next few years of my life for myself if you can decide how it's all going to go, just like that."

His voice was too curt, and he didn't know why he was tense in the first place. Why he cared what this woman—plain by his usual standards, and why was that so hard to remember when he looked at her?—thought about him. Especially because she was probably right.

His twin brother Jonah was the magnate, he was the dilettante. Or so Jonah had informed him the last time they'd spoken.

"But I'll still be here," she said, her voice low and easy, but not quite happy, snapping him back from yet another unpleasant contemplation of his strained relationship with his brother. Then she laughed, and he felt it like a rush of something carbonated, washing over him. "I'll be right here, trading concerned glances with every person who walks by because we've all known each other since birth. I'll learn how to age into my old maid status gracefully, and stop trying to date the few single men left who haven't already dated my friends. I already dress like my mother, as you so thoughtfully pointed out this morning. I'll become her sooner rather than later, ranting about the Crawfords and shushing boisterous children like a librarian except in the middle of Main Street, and you know what?"

He didn't think she knew that her cheeks were flushed with that tell-tale color, that her eyes were brilliant, that she looked more alive, and more beautiful, than he could have imagined possible. He felt that kick inside, in his gut and high in his chest, and he knew what it meant. What it was. However little he wanted it.

He'd be damned.

But she was still talking.

"This is a good life," she said quietly, with great conviction, and he believed her. "I might not have everything I want, but I'm happy. And it wouldn't kill you to let us build that museum, because what do you care, in the end? This is nothing more than a little side project for you to play with between acts of corporate dominance."

Jasper forgot about his beer. He saw nothing but Chelsea. He wanted nothing but Chelsea. He couldn't keep himself from grinning.

"This is it, Triple C."

She blinked. "What?"

He poked his finger down into the table between them.

"This moment, right here. This is that pivotal moment where you get to decide what kind of woman you are. What kind of life you want to live."

"I'm thirty years old," she said dryly. "I'm a well-established high school history teacher in the rural community where I was born. I'm pretty sure this is my life."

Jasper flipped his hand over and let it lie there, open, and he saw the way her throat moved, how she stared at it, as if she could feel the same pull he did.

"You can be this old maid creature you keep talking about," he said. "You can live it the way it is in your head, the way you see it all unfolding. Wearin' your mama's clothes and giving a shit what all these people think of you."

"Of course I care. I've known them all since birth." Her chin rose higher. "I like them. Most of the time."

"Do they get to decide who you are or do you?"

She stared at him for a long moment, so long he thought he'd read this wrong, read *her* wrong. But then she shifted slightly, and he was relieved. Maybe too relieved.

"What's the other option?" she asked.

"That's the fun one." He grinned. "You can be the woman who gets on the back of the bike of a man she met this morning, and lets whatever happens next, happen. No matter who's watching, even if they've known you since birth."

Her hands twitched near her glass, but she still sat there, tight and frozen, as if she was afraid to move.

"To be clear," she said, in a very, very prissy voice that he was starting to understand meant Chelsea at her most nervous, "this is you propositioning me?" Her voice squeaked slightly on *propositioning,* and his grin widened. "At five-fifteen on a Monday evening two tables away from my dentist?"

"Oh, yeah, that's definitely what this is," he agreed, and thought he might lose it when her eyes went molten. "All you have to do is decide."

She licked her lips, he felt it like she'd kicked him, and then she blew out a breath like her lungs hurt.

"Well," she said, softly. "That's not really much of a decision, is it?"

And he experienced a stabbing moment of perfect fear that he knew he'd have to face later, when his mind worked again the way it was supposed to, when he was free of this spell she'd cast without him even noticing—

But then she leaned in close and slipped her hand into his.

Chapter Four

OUT ON MAIN Street again, Jasper climbed on his bike and started it up with a big growl of its powerful engine, then looked over his shoulder at Chelsea with his clever eyebrows raised, daring her.

He didn't think she'd do it, she realized.

And if she was honest, neither did she.

His eyes were that curious shade of hazel that made her think of sunshine and toffee, caramel and whiskey, sweetness and sin all at once, and they were fixed on her with so much *heat*. So much *intent*. And she knew he was right. This was her moment, here and now. She could seize it or she could hide from it, but he'd laid out the consequences of both of those choices on the table between them in the saloon in that stark, matter-of-fact way of his that his grin softened but didn't sweep away. Like he was her own, personal prophet, straddling a silver motorcycle on a gleaming fall evening, tempting her toward the kind of wickedness she'd only ever dreamed about before.

She'd dreamed about so many things, and done none of

them, because she'd spent her whole life taking the safe route, the expected path, the dutiful road. She'd pretended that being a coward deep down where it counted was a virtue. She'd let the fact she was afraid keep her from, well, everything. She'd never explored the world. She hadn't applied anywhere but Bozeman for college, even though she kept a private journal filled with dreams about magical, far-off cities: New York. Paris. London. Hell, even Seattle, the nearest big city, had seemed too big and too far for her. She'd only dated boys and then men she'd known would ask nothing of her, who she'd thought she could slot right into the life she already knew so well and help her keep herself safe in the role she'd been handed so long ago. Hadn't Tod simply been more of the same?

She'd been hiding all her life.

But somehow this man—this architect of her mother's latest despair and she knew she should heed that, or at least care about it more than she did in this moment—*saw* her. Straight through her, inside of her, to all those things she'd packed away years ago and told herself were for someone else. Those crazy dreams. That wildness she'd thought she couldn't have. The secret Chelsea Collier no one had ever known existed except her.

It was as exhilarating as it was terrifying, flashing through her like an electrical storm.

Chelsea took a deep, shaky breath. Then another. She knew there were eyes on her, approving and judgmental in equal measure, from every part of Main Street. She didn't look around to confirm it; she knew. She could *feel* them, just as she was sure she could feel her own mother's glare from as far away as Crawford House way up in the foothills, trying to bend Chelsea back into obedient shape from all those miles away.

But instead, Chelsea met Jasper's 100-proof gaze and told herself it didn't make her feel the least bit drunk.

"I'm not getting on that thing without a helmet," she told him.

Prim and proper, as if she was discussing a ladies luncheon instead of… all the things that swirled between her and this man—this stranger—and made her feel wild and unmanageable and *alive.*

Alive, like she'd been faking it all this time. Every day of her life, until this one.

Jasper grinned, then reached down into one of the side compartments on his sleek and sexy machine and pulled out a little leather thing that she supposed was a helmet. Technically. Though she couldn't imagine what good leather would do if they—

But she wasn't going to think about consequences. Not tonight.

"Here," he said, handing it to her. "But you're going to have to let your hair down, Rapunzel."

Chelsea's throat was too dry. Her fingers shook. But she reached up and released the clip that held her chignon in place, then let her hair tumble down, aware as she did it that she was trespassing into the kind of feminine territory she'd always thought she was too boring, too responsible, to take part in. She'd watched girls do this all her life, and so, somehow, she couldn't help herself tonight, given the opportunity to act like someone else. Like the Chelsea he seemed to see, instead of the Chelsea all the other men she'd dated had known perfectly well would never do anything like this.

As her thick, blonde hair fell down to her shoulders, she shook her head to make it swirl around her, then ran her fingers through it in an age-old gesture she'd never understood the full power of until now.

Until Jasper Flint sat on a gorgeous bike and watched her with the narrow, hungry focus of a predator, that hard grin of his a threat and a promise, reverberating in her like a chord struck long and deep.

She buckled the leather helmet beneath her chin, then leaned in when he beckoned and let him check its tightness. Her knees felt wobbly and there was a hunger carving out an empty space in her belly. Lower. She felt his breath on her face, his strong fingers brushing against her skin, and shook, deep inside.

"Get on," he said, his voice gravelly, and she didn't have to be an expert on men to know that meant he was as affected by this as she was. That made her feel small and powerful at once. Almost dizzy. "There's a lot of carousing yet to do before we lose the light."

"I'm not much of a carouser," she told him, very seriously, because she thought he ought to know the truth before this went too far. "In the sense that I've never caroused in my entire life, by any definition of the word. You might want to adjust your expectations."

"That's not how I roll, Triple C." His grin went wolfish. "I've never seen a boundary yet I didn't like to push. You might want to let go of your expectations altogether."

He made that sound like the most delicious, most dangerous prospect imaginable. And Chelsea decided she wanted nothing more than to let him push every single boundary he discovered in her. No matter what happened. No matter what it cost.

She climbed up behind him on the bike, carefully, feeling ungainly and graceless, like a single wrong move might topple the whole thing over, crushing them beneath—

"You're not going to break it," he said over his shoulder as she slid into place, feeling off-balance and unsafe, and not in a fun way. "But you'll fall right off if you don't hold on."

"I am holding on."

She had a death grip on the back of her seat, and she felt foolish sitting there, splayed open behind him and red with uncertainty, for everyone to see.

"You're missing the point," he said, and did she imagine there was something gentler in his voice then, winding through her and making it easier to breathe? "Why do you think a man rides a bike?"

"A death wish, presumably," she snapped back at him, too overwhelmed to be anything but snappish, and maybe slightly hysterical while she was at it. "Also, they're loud."

"Sure," he said, shrugging, and she had the impression of his laughter, though when he shifted in his seat, all she saw was the firm line of his distracting mouth and perfect jaw, and no laughter at all. "But there are other, better reasons."

He reached back and tugged her arms around his chest, then yanked her close, so she lost her rigid place completely and just… slid into him, the most tender part of her crushed against his behind and her breasts flat against the perfect, smooth wall of his back.

She made a shocked, small little noise, and felt the rumble of his laughter then, radiating through his strong back, his wide shoulders, the smoothly-muscled torso where her hands rested. *This is too intimate,* she thought, scandalized and vulnerable at once. The powerful machine beneath her, this equally powerful man in front of her, sitting right there between her legs—

"This is one of the best reasons," he rumbled at her, low and hot, and she could feel his voice almost as well as she could hear it, moving in him and then in her, shaking her apart in an entirely new way. "Hold on tight."

Then he kicked the bike into gear, and took off, the motorcycle like a gleaming, muscular bullet into the coming dusk, headed out of town in a low, sleek growl.

And Chelsea simply held on tight, the way he'd told her to, and surrendered.

They rode for a long time.

The world narrowed down to the roar of the bike and the wind against her face. The man she clung to, and the heat of his broad, muscled back. As the light started to sneak toward the far off hills, he stopped, high up on one of the Copper Mountain overlooks.

It took Chelsea a moment to come back to earth. To remember herself and peel herself away from him, then climb off the motorcycle so he could, too. She unbuckled her leather helmet and placed it carefully—too carefully—on the seat she'd just abandoned.

She felt exposed and scared—though it was a different kind of scared, she recognized. Not her usual *head in the sand* version. This was more the *I might explode* kind, and she didn't know what to do about it, so she turned away from him and looked out over the familiar stretch of land before her instead, turning red and gold in the light of the setting sun.

"Legend has it that the first settlers here believed there was copper in these mountains because of sunsets like this one," she heard herself say, though she hardly recognized her own voice, small and reverent, scared and soft. "They thought it was a sign."

Jasper moved to stand behind her, and she could feel that intense blast of his heat she'd come to depend on during the long ride, looping around and around through the fields and into the hills. It emanated from him, like he was his own furnace, and she felt cold without it.

She thought she might die if he touched her. She knew she'd die if he didn't. She felt restless, shivery—and the feel of him was still pressed into her, like he'd branded her, all that smooth, male muscle, that heft and power.

Chelsea wished they were still riding. That she was still touching him. That they could have gone on like that forever.

"I stopped here when I was riding through," he said, his own voice different, like he felt it too. "Almost a year ago. We'd decided to sell the company, and I was trying to figure out what came next."

"I think a lot of men in your position figure that out on private Caribbean islands," she said dryly. "Not in rural Montana."

"If I liked men in my position, I'd probably still be one of them."

She wanted to look back at him, to gauge the expression on his face, but she was afraid to move. To break this spell, whatever it was.

"Chelsea." Not *Triple C.* Not now. Like it meant something, the way he said her name. The way it cut into the twilight that settled around them.

And then he waited.

She knew that's what he was doing. Just standing there,

waiting for her to make the choice. The way he had three times already now. Outside the saloon. At the table. And before she got on his bike.

My choice, she thought fiercely. *This is* mine.

And so she turned around to look at him, standing there like something she might have conjured up in her head, so impossibly beautiful in the last of the day's light it made her pulse pound. The reds and golds teased over him, making him that much more compelling, like he was truly that bronze she'd imagined him.

She didn't care who she was or who she was supposed to be, Chelsea thought then. She simply wanted him, and nothing else mattered.

So she moved closer, stretching up to loop her arms around his neck as if it was the most natural thing in the world. He traced lazy shapes over her upper arms, and the smile he gave her then seemed carved from stone, sharp and hot.

"Is this where the carousing starts?" she asked, amazed that her voice was so husky. Amazed that the sound of it didn't embarrass her.

She felt like she was alone in the world with this man, and she loved it. She wanted it. Him. Nothing but him—whatever that meant.

"If you think you can handle it."

"I know I can't," she murmured, his mouth so close now, his head bent to hers, his hands moving over her shoulders to sink into her hair and tug her head back. "But I'm a quick learner."

"Hallelujah," he muttered, and then he kissed her.

Chelsea had been kissed before, even well, she would have said.

But Jasper was a revelation.

He kissed her the way he'd driven them on his bike, with an ease and a skill that combined into something liquid and powerful, driving her straight out of her head. He took her mouth like it was his, like she was his and always had been, and he tasted like fire and whiskey.

And she *wanted.* She *yearned.*

His hands sunk deep in her hair, holding her head right where he wanted it, while he bent her back and commanded her mouth with his own. And she couldn't seem to get close enough. She couldn't seem to *think.* She simply exploded into his hands, pressed herself against his body as close as she could get, lost herself in the wildfire he kicked up so easily, the sweet, hot burn.

He pulled back and muttered something under his breath, then smoothed a hand over her hair, his breath ragged as he studied her face. He frowned at her.

"What the hell was that?"

She didn't know how she could stand there with his hands on her, kicking up so many brushfires she didn't think she'd ever put them all out again. She wasn't sure her legs worked any longer, and it felt like there was champagne in her veins, bubbling everywhere, thick and sweet and enough to make her head spin.

And he was looking at her like *she'd* stunned *him.*

Chelsea thought this might be what it felt like to fly like the eagles that had soared overhead on their ride up here, so bold and free.

"I thought I wasn't your type," she said.

That wolfish crook of his lips. "You most definitely are not."

He traced the ruffled placket of her shirt as if it fascinated him, and her heart hit so hard against her chest she thought it might cripple her, but he only swept that damned finger up and down and back again, as if he didn't notice how close he was to her breasts or how desperately she wanted his touch—so desperately she felt bright red and bursting with it.

"Well," she said huffily, as if none of that was happening and he was simply another surly teen slinking into her classroom for detention. "You're certainly not my type. I prefer the gainfully employed, for one thing. Safe, steady, and sturdy."

That grin widened. "Sounds like you're talking about support beams. I think someone needs to mess you up a bit, darlin', if that's the kind of thing you're looking for in bed. You're missing all the fun."

"I hate mess."

"Then you shouldn't kiss like that. It's distracting."

"I don't kiss like anything!" She blinked, considering that. "Do I?"

"You kiss like a very loose woman with a very long night ahead of her," he told her, and his finger crooked between two of the buttons of her shirt, which she only registered for a scant moment before he yanked her close to him again, plastering her against him, making her moan like the loose woman he'd just described.

Making her wish she was, because maybe then they'd already be naked.

"That's me," she lied breathlessly. "I dance on tables and engage in very long, very loose nights at least three times a week. I'm bad to the bone."

"I like that about you."

And this time, when he took her mouth, he lifted her up, wrapping her around him and holding her there as if she weighed nothing at all. He pressed her against the unmistakable jut of his arousal, and she shivered, then moved restlessly against him, trying to get closer—trying to do something with that terrible, all-consuming *ache* that she thought might eat her alive.

Her legs were locked around his waist and his arms were around her, and she felt like she was flying again, like they were still on his bike and this was more noise, more speed, more of that intense rush, ruining her for anything else. She knew it.

She couldn't seem to care. Or stop.

So it almost hurt her when he did. When he put her back on the ground, very carefully, and then stepped away from her.

"Don't look at me like that," he gritted out. "Or I swear to god, I'll take you right here."

She couldn't think of a single reason why he shouldn't do exactly that, which must have shown on her face, and he cursed. Then let out a laugh.

"Come on," he said, gruff and needy. "I'm either taking you home, or I'm taking you to my bed, where I might not let you go for a long time. Your choice, Chelsea. But I'm not doing this on the side of a mountain where anyone could drive by and see us. I'm not an animal."

"What if I want you to be?" she asked. She didn't know where it came from. His gaze took on that narrow, hungry gleam, and she felt it turn molten inside of her, promising all manner of dark, delectable things. "What if you make me feel like one?"

"Careful what you wish for," he rasped out. "Your home or mine, Triple C. Decide."

But of course, she already had.

Chapter Five

THE LAST TIME Jasper had brought a woman home, that home had been his absurdly ostentatious mansion in Dallas's Preston Hollow neighborhood, an enclave of the very rich that he'd aspired to ever since his daddy had driven him through it when he was a kid and told him Flints would never be good enough to live in a place like it.

He'd wasted more time than he cared to think about proving the old man wrong.

The home he brought Chelsea to was a far cry from that monstrosity.

He pushed his way inside the old, ornate door and slapped at the wall switch, aware as the vast space blazed with the sudden light that he hadn't really thought this through. He didn't know what this cavernous loft he'd only just started pulling together looked like to anyone else. He only knew what it represented to him.

His dreams, not his father's. *His* taste, not the outlandishly expensive opinions of his ex-wife via Dallas's snootiest interior decorator, who'd made such a point of sniffing over every last hint that Jasper was as uncouth and untutored as suspected. He'd ended up feeling like a bull in a china shop house, unwelcome in his own damned home, and he'd vowed when he left that he'd never subject himself to that again. He'd decided to live up on the top floor of the train depot mostly because of the light. It poured in from all sides, and there were mountains in every direction. It made his heart feel too big for his chest. It felt right.

But that didn't mean Chelsea would like it.

Jasper really didn't want to think about how important it was to him that she did.

He stayed quiet as she walked inside. That deliciously frilly shirt of hers was untucked now and her wavy blonde hair scraped at her shoulders, hanging in a tousled mess around her head, and he was lost for a breath or two in the rhythm of her hips, sensual and enticing, as she moved further into the great room.

She stopped, her heels loud against the old floors, and turned in a slow circle.

He wondered how it looked through those Big Sky eyes of hers. The remnants of his old life he'd only just unloaded into the room, having made only a few gestures toward separating it all into a makeshift bedroom, dining area, living room. The standing lamps that stood here and there, making the light more of a golden glow. The big brass bed on the far wall, and the gigantic mirror that he'd bought over the objections of his ex-wife, and had taken when he'd left her that monster of a house and all the fussy, asinine things she'd filled it with. Including a new oil man, he'd heard through the grapevine, which was all she'd ever wanted.

Good riddance, he thought, without the slightest shred of bitterness or rancor, which was one among the many ways he knew he never should have married Marlene in the first place. She could keep her monument to tackiness and the *nouveau riche* lifestyle she loved so much. Jasper didn't want any part of it.

What was here in this space was what mattered to him. It was excruciating to discover that Chelsea did, too, this woman who'd shown up out of nowhere this morning and tilted his world in a whole new direction. It was an uncomfortable sensation, but he let it wash through him, and he waited for her verdict.

"I feel like I'm standing in the attic of a very old, very eclectic palace," she said, her voice a lovely thread of sound in the great space, and when she turned to him, her whole face was lit up and her blue eyes sparkled. "Or some kind of eccentric museum."

Jasper decided, then and there, that he would keep her.

But first, he thought he might die if he didn't find a way to taste her. To discover every inch of that body of hers that she hid away in those hideous clothes—but he'd held her in his arms, felt her pressed tight to his back, and he knew better. He knew that what she hid away was far better than what she showed.

If he didn't get inside her soon, he thought he might rip apart, from the inside out.

He prowled toward her, taking a deep satisfaction in the way her eyes widened in a kind of sensual alarm that told him everything he needed to know about her supposed career as a bad girl. She was backing up, moving away from him, and he bet she didn't even know it—a bet he won when she backed right into the side of his bed and let out a startled little yelp.

"Oh," she said.

Breathless and wide-eyed and his, he thought. Utterly his, every delectable inch of her.

"Oh?" He was teasing her as he closed the distance between them, mocking her gently, and he had the pleasure of watching her shiver.

But she only swallowed, hard and loud, her eyes on him as if she was the one who was mesmerized. God, the things he wanted to do to her.

"I wasn't kidding about the jeans," he told her, when he could reach over and start to work on that shirt of hers, those silly ruffles that wound down over the swell of her breasts and her belly beneath.

"I'm not buying something that shows my ass just because you think I should," she snapped at him, but there was no heat in it, and he knew that was because he was tugging open the shirt and baring her perfect breasts to his view, enough to fill his palms and swelling against a lovely bra in a pale blue shade that made him want, desperately, to know every last one of her secrets.

"I hate your clothes, Triple C," he whispered, leaning in to deliver each word against the softness of her skin, to feel that exquisite shiver of hers himself.

He pushed the shirt off her shoulders and let her deal with it while he made short work of her belt. He shoved the ill-fitting black mess down from her hips and then sucked in a breath, because she was even better than he'd imagined. He helped her step out of the pants as they pooled around her ankles, and then he kept holding her hand while he eased back so he could look at her.

He was a goner. She was perfect.

All those curves, lovingly held in those scraps of pale blue lace. Her long legs, sweet hips, gently rounded belly. That messy, just-out-of-bed hair that he could still feel slide through his fingers like a rough silk, scented like almonds and cream, all around her lovely face. And that mouth of hers that had made him uncomfortably hard when she'd been dressed like a dour old matron and now, wearing nothing but lingerie and very high heels that were made for his favorite kind of dirty, imaginative sinning—

He *hurt*.

"Get on the bed," he ordered her, his voice almost angry with the violence of the need in him, the pounding, relentless grip of it.

"You're looking at me like I'm a ghost," she whispered,

and he could see everything she felt on her face.

Reserve, uncertainty. Lust and desire. Need. Fear.

"I'm looking at you like I'm about to eat you alive," he retorted, unable to keep the tension from his voice, the need. "Because I am."

He watched her shake even as he felt it in her fingers, and then she tugged her hand from his and obeyed him, sliding all of that soft, feminine deliciousness into the center of his brand new, ridiculously large and pretentious bed, that no one had been in but him. Twice.

And then he stripped off his own clothes with laughable speed and all the grace of a very, very lucky teenage boy, before he crawled up and joined her.

He could see her pulse rocket against the delicate skin of her neck. He thought that if her eyes got any wider he might fall in, and he'd never in his life wanted anything more than he wanted to please this woman, so much and so deep she'd be as addicted to him as he was very much afraid he was to her.

He stretched out over her, every sharp intake of breath she took like music to his ears, every restless twist of her hips and shiver that traveled the length of her body, and he was grinning by the time he took her hands and stretched them out above her, wrapping them around the brass rails that formed his headboard.

"Hold on, darlin'," he murmured, a dark promise he had every intention of keeping. "I expect this is going to get a little bit crazy."

He wasn't kidding.

Chelsea's hands dug into the brass headboard while Jasper settled that powerful body of his over hers. Then she gripped it even harder, because he leaned in close, and used his mouth.

That mouth.

He spread a raging, impossible fire everywhere he touched, and he took his sweet time doing it. He tasted the line of her neck, the ridge of her collarbone. He held her breasts in his hands, then licked his way into the hollow between them, making her moan and thrash, yet he made no move to take her bra off. He tested every inch of the belly she'd previously thought was her worst feature, growling out his intensely male approval directly into her skin, so she could feel the curve of his smile pressed there below her navel.

Then he moved even lower, holding her hips in his hands and exploring every inch of what lay between, using his mouth, his jaw, the whole of him, like he really was a wild animal and he was scent-marking her. Tasting her and changing her. Then he learned her thighs, her calves, all the way down to those damned shoes, which he tugged off her feet and admired before tossing them aside.

Crouched down at her feet, his hands on her skin and

that dark heat making his hazel eyes gleam gold, she thought he looked like a panther. Something as sleek and menacing and deliciously dangerous as that bike he rode so well.

"Do I get to touch you?" she asked, in a voice that didn't sound like hers at all. It came from that lick of fire, that dancing need, that coiled in her and became her. Took her over until there was nothing in the whole world but this man. This bed.

This.

"You'll get your turn," he said, sounding amused, and that, too, was like a blaze inside of her, making her stomach twist and her breasts seem to swell against the lace of her bra. Making her feel slippery and swollen and needier, somehow, than she'd known was possible.

But then, this man was revelation upon revelation. Every moment, every touch.

He prowled back up over her the way he'd stalked her across the grand stretch of this floor he'd made his home, and Chelsea gripped the bedrails and watched, her breath loud and unmistakable between them as he dispensed with her panties. Then she released her hold when he moved to her bra.

And then there was nothing between them except all of that wild heat.

She didn't think, she just reached for him.

Finally, she traced those mouthwatering ridges on his steel-hewn torso that had stunned her this morning, that she'd felt move beneath her palms on that long ride tonight. Finally, she leaned forward and lost herself in all his heat, his hardness, all those fascinating planes and muscles that made him something like steel wrapped in velvet.

"You're not built like an executive," she murmured, and felt his laughter move inside his hard chest even as she heard it above her, around her.

"We Flints are more laborers than liege lords," he said. "Can't help it. Not one of us does too well behind a desk."

She filed that away, and then gasped when he tossed her back down on the bed, his easy expression gone like it had never been. He was all heat and dark intent, and even while she trembled, she wanted him in ways she didn't understand. She watched as he reached over to a box beside the bed, rummaged around in it, then came back with a condom. She wanted to *do* something while he rolled it on that long, hard length of his that made her mouth go dry, but she felt pinned in place as surely as if he'd held her down. He didn't have to; his gaze did it—too bright, too intense, making her feel as if he'd wrapped those steel arms around her chest and squeezed.

And then he was settling himself between her legs, and the hardest part of him was nudging against her molten center.

Chelsea had never felt like this. Lit up, made new.

"I thought I was promised carousing," she said, daring and reckless and it felt *good,* like flying down the side of

Copper Mountain on the back of his motorcycle, like laughing while his hazel eyes held hers. Like him. "This appears to be textbook missionary position."

"This is called taking the edge off," he replied, dropping down, his head next to hers, his arms holding her tight against him. "I think you can suffer through it."

"I guess," she said, and sighed as if it was a stretch for her, but even as she did, he thrust himself into her.

And everything splintered. Changed forever.

Caught fire.

It was slick, hard, *perfect*. It was unbelievable.

She thought she said his name. Maybe he said hers. Maybe there was nothing at all anymore but that searing fusion, so deep inside of her she didn't think she'd ever be the same again. She didn't *want* to be the same.

And then he began to move, and everything shattered again.

Then again.

He set a wild pace, a glorious rhythm, and Chelsea met him as if she'd done this a thousand times, as if she'd been put on this earth to dance like this, with this man. As if her previous experiences didn't seem black and white and pointless with each expert surge, each rock of his hips, each utterly insane movement.

And all the while, his mouth was at her neck, her lips. Urging her on, making her gasp. He muttered filthy and beautiful words, like a thread of darkest poetry straight into her ears, her sex. He called her carnal and amazing and all manner of things she'd never imagined she could be, and she believed him.

She was all those things, when he touched her. When he moved over her, in her, dark and graceful, sleek and perfect, as if he'd been crafted by some benevolent god for exactly this purpose.

She felt her back arch, her hips reach for his of their own accord. Felt a wildness like a panic, a wave, crash over her.

"Yes," he said, his voice something like harsh, and then he issued a series of dark commands, one after the next, and she obeyed.

She burst into a thousand fiery pieces. She screamed. And she held him tight when he followed her, whispering her name like a prayer.

Chapter Six

JASPER TOOK HER home when the night was starting to edge over into the start of another deep blue morning, in a Range Rover that purred quietly up the long and twisting drive that branched off of Black Bart Road and led up the hill to Crawford House.

"Black Bart?" Jasper asked when he saw the street sign. "That doesn't sound like the kind of name people generally bestow upon the more revered members of society."

"I mentioned he was an ass." Chelsea laughed. "It was only when his descendants wanted to lord it over everyone else in this valley that they started making noise about social classes. Barton Crawford liked being rich, period."

It seemed to her that Jasper went very still beside her, or the air changed.

"I know the type," he said after a moment, in a low voice that made Chelsea frown—but then they were turning off the road onto the unpaved drive that looked exactly the same as it did it all those ancient pictures Mama had framed and hanging in the house, with the forest pressing in on all sides and quick glimpses of clearings and pastures as they wound their way toward the historic front door.

Where Chelsea's mother was probably sitting up waiting, simmering in outrage and wrapped in her years of disappointment like a woolen throw against the night's chill.

She knew she should feel something about that—anxiety, even panic—but she didn't. She couldn't. Not yet.

Not while they were still cocooned together in the quiet warmth of the Range Rover's front seat that smelled of leather and pine, his large hand so easy on her leg, like they'd done all of this a trillion times before. Like they *belonged.*

He felt like fate, and she knew better than that. But she soaked in it even so, while he took the curves of the long drive with the quiet competence he'd showed in everything else he did, and she pretended that she was fated to be someone other than who she'd always been—until tonight.

Jasper had been as good as his word. He'd "taken the edge off," and then he'd taken her again. And again. He'd feasted on her, let her return the favor, and then he'd done things to her she'd never imagined she'd do at all, much less like as much as she had. And she'd gloried in every moment. In every stroke of his bold possession, in every heated whisper, in all of that wild, intense passion that she could still feel simmering inside of her, a flickering flame she didn't think would ever go out again.

She hadn't wanted to leave. She didn't want this night to end, to have to force herself back into her tiny and safe little life. Not now that she knew how it could be, if things were different. If *she* was different.

Jasper was talented and imaginative, demanding and sure, and even thinking about the things that had happened in that gigantic bed of his made her core throb and then ache all over again. It made her wonder how she'd never known that she had all of that inside of her—that wantonness, that abandon. That shuddering need that she'd explored again and again beneath his hands, his mouth, that knowing gaze of his.

Like he knew exactly what was inside of her. Like he could see it.

"Thank you," she said softly when he pulled up to the house. Mama hadn't left the lights on, which could be either a good or bad sign. Chelsea didn't know which, though she supposed she'd find out soon enough. "I can honestly say that in all the years I've lived here, I've never had a night quite like this one."

"Marietta men must be damned fools."

"I didn't say I didn't have nights that were similar in many respects. No need to get *quite* such a big head."

"You know that every single thing you think shows on your face, don't you?" He reached over and brushed a lazy finger over one cheek, then the other, and that current between them sizzled all over again, sparking like it was new. He grinned when her breath caught, like he felt it move in him, too. "You're like a billboard. I can read every thought and feeling you have. Right here."

She shouldn't find that charming; she should be horrified. Alarmed, certainly. But for some reason, she smiled.

"You can't."

"Which is only one of the many ways I know I rocked your world, Triple C. Aside from being there, doing the rocking, I mean."

"You're an insufferably conceited man." But she was still smiling, even wider now, like these were love words. Incidental poetry in that low growl of a voice.

He shook his head, his gaze intent on hers, then dropping down to her lips.

"It's that prissy little voice coming out of that mouth of yours. It's so damned hot." It took a long time for him to drag his gaze back up to hers, and by the time he did, she'd succumbed to that heat again. It flashed over her, drugging and deep. "You're the kind of girl who could start a bar fight."

Chelsea was almost positive that was an insult and that she should be offended. Shouldn't she? But she'd spent thirty years being widely regarded as the sort of woman who might faint at the idea of *entering* a bar. A kind of latter day Puritan, by default. The kind of woman, or so she'd heard through the grapevine, that men cheated on because she *felt too much* and they were afraid to admit to her that they *had darker needs.*

The kind of solid, bland, invisible woman absolutely no

one in her right mind would ever choose to be. Who Chelsea had simply *become* without meaning to, sometime in high school, and had been stuck with ever since.

The notion that she might be the kind of femme fatale-like creature who drove men to get into brawls? To act like fools, like she could make them lose their heads? Obviously, she should be appalled at the notion. But there was that part of her—the part that reveled in feeling that surge of feminine power from deep inside, the part that felt like joy—that exulted in the idea.

"What would you do?" she asked. His expression turned quizzical. "If I started a bar fight?"

His lips crooked, and she knew how they tasted now. The magic they could do.

"Oh," he said, his voice thick with Texas and a certain male confidence she should find offensive, she knew she should, "I'd handle it." The look he shot her then was level, the faint amusement in those bright hazel depths intoxicating. "But then you and I would have a pretty serious conversation."

He leaned in closer then, cupping the back of her head in his hand and pulling her mouth to his. He kissed her, hard and consuming, as if the night was just getting started. And she wished it was, harder than she'd ever wished anything else.

"My God," she whispered, when she could speak again, because the darkness outside the car was bluer by the moment, and she had a real life waiting for her no matter how hard she pretended otherwise. "I have to teach in the morning."

"I hate to break this to you, darlin', but it's already morning."

Chelsea glanced at her watch, then shuddered. "I have to go."

His smile was the most beautiful thing she'd ever seen, and she knew she was hoarding it even as it happened—tucking the image of it away somewhere deep inside, in case this was the last time she ever saw it. She told herself that didn't hurt to think like that, that *bittersweet* was a good thing.

It meant something worthwhile had finally happened to her.

"Go." His voice was a low scrape that worked in her like another touch of those talented hands of his, that punch of giddy fire, the same kick in her pulse. "Before I change my mind and keep you."

It was only a line. She knew that. But it still burst inside of her, bright and sharp, and she knew she'd cling to it when he was gone. Maybe for the rest of her sensible, solid, old maid's life, right here in this house she was fairly certain was her destiny, as she slowly and irrevocably turned into her mother.

Chelsea made herself climb out of his car though it was by far the hardest thing she'd ever done, and she liked that he waited there as she walked to her door, watching intently like he thought the mountain lions might swoop in and get her on the short walk to safety.

The trouble was, she liked it all. Everything about this man who should have been her enemy. *Too much.*

And as she opened the door and slipped back in to her comfortable life and the consequences she'd surely have to suffer for what she'd done tonight, Chelsea still felt Jasper's hard mouth on hers and the hot brand of his possession like an ache inside of her, and she knew it was worth it.

Whatever happened next, she didn't regret a single second of this night.

Not one second.

She made it through a particularly chilly breakfast a few hours later in the face of Mama's furious silence. The Silent Treatment was her mother's weapon of choice. Usually, Mama trotted it out and Chelsea fell all over herself trying to fix whatever was wrong. Cajoling and even begging, until Mama could be coaxed into discussing whatever it was she was angry about. It was better to grovel a little than to suffer through the angry silence, which Chelsea could remember Mama unleashing on the entire family for weeks at a time when she'd been a kid. It was part of the game.

But the Chelsea Collier who had roared off on a stranger's motorcycle and found herself in his bed all night didn't want to play that game. Not today. If Mama wanted silence, she could do silence. It was better than the recriminations that were sure to follow.

She stood for what felt like hours in her shower, pretending the hot water was as restorative as a night's sleep, then found she hated all of her usual work outfits when she looked for something to wear. She might not want to prance around with her ass on display the way Jasper had told her she should, but she discovered that after last night, it turned out she had a whole wealth of feminine vanity she'd never paid the slightest bit of attention to before. Whatever else happened today, she didn't want to face it while dressed like a woman twice her age.

It took some digging, but she found a black dress Jenny had talked her into buying in Bozeman once on one of her wedding-planning expeditions, but which Chelsea had banished to the depths of her closet. It was just *too much,* she remembered thinking. But she pulled it on today, and liked the way the soft material flowed around her. It was feminine and flattering, skimming over her curves without calling too much attention to them and then flaring out on its way to her knees. She started to twist her hair back, but stopped, letting it fall to her shoulders instead, because it seemed to go better with the dress. A pair of low heels with a delicate ankle strap and she was ready for school—and dressed, she thought, like she thought she deserved to be considered pretty as well as competent.

Because she did. And she was. And she didn't know why that had never occurred to her before.

And she couldn't think of a better outcome from her first and only one night stand than to hold herself in higher esteem because of it.

Mama harrumphed as she passed her on her way out the door, and then scowled when Chelsea only grinned at her.

And then she set off to face her fate.

The long drive down into town from Crawford House was stunningly beautiful that morning, the way it always was, with the mountains and the sky and the clear air in all directions, and Chelsea put her windows down despite the chill of the morning and breathed it deep into her lungs.

She'd never been involved in one of Marietta's scandals, except by default. She'd been the pitiable creature who that otherwise nice Tod had betrayed, the sad sack girlfriend who couldn't hold on to her man—never the scarlet woman. She found that on some level, she was looking forward to it.

At least it was something new.

And unlike what had happened on Tod's back deck in July, this time, it was actually about her.

She didn't expect to see Jasper again. She told herself she was fine with that as she pulled into the parking lot at the high school. She was a grown woman—she knew how things worked even if she'd never worked them herself before. Hadn't most women her age collected a number of these nights by now? The good news was, she didn't have to go to any great lengths to avoid Jasper in the aftermath of their night together. She'd never spent much time in Grey's

Saloon, so their paths were unlikely to cross aside from the usual nod and wave in public spaces.

You can handle this, she told herself briskly. *People do it all the time.*

Chelsea jumped slightly when she heard a car door slam nearby, jerking back into the here and now to see Gemma Clayton, a fellow teacher in the history department, heading toward the school building. She waved and smiled with genuine pleasure, and knew it was time to get on with the rest of her life.

She doubted she'd have to interact much with Jasper Flint ever again.

Chelsea got out of her car and started across the parking lot toward the smiling, waiting Gemma and the school doors, telling herself that what she felt then was nothing more than the cool morning air, the crisp fall weather, and not a sharp shot of something hollow, straight into her heart.

"Do you have a minute?"

Chelsea smiled automatically as she glanced up to see Sharla Dickinson, the high school principal, standing in the door of her classroom.

"I was about to head home for the day," she said, packing up her bag as she spoke, shoving a whole stack of student essays in with rather less care than she usually took. "But sure, I have a minute. Even two."

She wanted nothing more than to drag herself home, crawl into her bed, and sleep until her alarm went off the next morning, but she didn't say that. She thought she'd done a decent job of pretending not to be dead on her feet all day—surely she could hold on for a few more minutes.

"I wonder if we need to talk," Sharla said, and the strange note in her voice made Chelsea pause, then search her boss's face.

"About?"

Sharla looked more uncomfortable than Chelsea had ever seen her. "I just think it's worth reiterating that while this is a small town, it's best for everyone—for the students in particular—if we keep our personal lives private."

Chelsea let out a startled laugh. "I agree completely, Sharla. Has there been some kind of incident?"

If she wasn't mistaken, Sharla, who had once faced down the angry father of a pregnant high school junior toting a shotgun without so much as breaking a sweat, was blushing. She opened her mouth as if to say something, but instead waved a hand at Chelsea. Or, more specifically, at her dress.

"Just look at you," she said, and then shook her head. "I don't like to listen to gossip, Chelsea—"

"Then don't."

Sharla sighed. "Is this going to be an issue?"

Chelsea straightened, and felt her chin tip up, which was never a great sign.

"If you mean, will I wear perfectly conservative dresses to

work, then the answer is yes. I very well might. Unless there's a new dress code that applies only to me?"

"You don't look like yourself," Sharla said gently.

She was about twice her age, now that Chelsea thought about it, and was wearing an outfit eerily similar to the one Chelsea had been sporting yesterday. Jasper had hit that nail on the head, she thought wryly. With his usual hard, unerring accuracy.

But she wasn't thinking about Jasper. That was an exercise in futility, and she was determined to be the kind of adventurous woman who had no time for the futile. She wanted to act the way she thought a woman like that would act: like she did such things *all the time* and it was all *no big deal.*

She kept chanting those phrases in her head, like they might stick.

But Sharla was still talking, a frown etched between her eyes. "I'm worried about you."

"Because I'm wearing a dress?"

"Because the Chelsea Collier I know never would have made a spectacle of herself in the middle of Main Street yesterday evening," Sharla said, and her voice wasn't at all accusing. It was *concerned.*

Which Chelsea found was maybe the most insulting of all.

"Sharla," she said, fighting to keep her voice calm, and happy that all her years of teaching teenagers made her able to do that to some degree, "correct me if I'm wrong, but doesn't Lewis own a motorcycle?"

"You know he does."

"And didn't I see you riding on the back of that motorcycle all the way down Main Street on the Fourth of July? The high school principal on a Harley, hanging on to her boyfriend's waist for everyone to see?"

"That's not really the point, and I think you know it."

Chelsea fantasized about her bed. The soft pillows, room to stretch out—God, she wanted to close her eyes for a while. A long while. She rubbed a hand over her face instead, and hoped that if she pretended she didn't have that pounding at her temples, it would go away.

"I don't have the slightest idea what your point is," she said honestly.

"You," Sharla said simply. "My point is you. When all of that unpleasantness happened this summer—"

"My boyfriend cheated on me and I caught him in the act." It felt liberating to simply *say* that. Not to mince around it with all of those euphemisms and *significant looks* for once. "I won't faint if we call it what it was."

"This is what I'm trying to say," Sharla said then. "When it happened you were horrified that you were suddenly the name on everyone's lips. But today, it's like you're proud of it. That change concerns me. It concerns me more that it *doesn't* seem to strike you as odd at all."

Chelsea wished she could say what she actually

thought—which was, simply, that comparing Tod Styles to Jasper Flint was like comparing a flashlight to the summer sun, and what did she care what people said about it? She wasn't horrified. At all.

But she doubted Sharla would understand that when she wasn't certain she did.

"He comes from a very different world," Sharla was saying, still frowning at Chelsea, her gaze direct and intent. And still so *concerned*.

"And I'm a simple, hometown girl who's easily made a fool of," Chelsea finished for her.

"I didn't say that," her boss said calmly. "But you had a big disappointment this summer and I'd hate to think this was some kind of reaction to that. Or that you threw yourself into something only to find you're in over your head."

It was one thing, Chelsea realized, for *her* to think that Jasper was out of her league and to caution herself against holding out any hope for anything more than the one night they'd had. It was something else entirely to have someone else think all of that and worse, that she was a naïve idiot who *Tod* had so destroyed that she'd tossed herself into the path of the romantic equivalent of a speeding train.

It took every bit of willpower she had to keep her temper under control. And to keep her mouth shut on a selection of inappropriate retorts, from a breezy *Oh, I was just using him for sex* to a snappier *The only thing that disappointed me this summer was that I'd ever suffered Tod's company in the first place.*

There was no point and anyway, this woman was her boss as much as she was a friend, it would behoove her to remember. Chelsea waited until she was sure she could control herself before she let herself speak.

"Maybe," she said kindly, very kindly, because she could see Sharla only wanted to help—that Sharla thought she *needed* help and was trying to give it despite the fact it made her uncomfortable—and that came from a good place no matter how it made her grit her teeth, "you don't know me as well as you think you do. Maybe no one does." She picked up her bag and looped it over her arm, then started toward the door, a silent announcement that she was done with this conversation. "And maybe that's something it's high time I changed."

Chapter Seven

JASPER DIDN'T KNOW what the hell he was doing, lurking around outside the high school like some kind of obsessed, insane stalker. But baffling though he might find his own behavior, he couldn't seem to help himself.

Besides, he told himself, stalkers would hide. Conceal themselves behind the hedges or something. They wouldn't stand there out in the open, leaning up against his Range Rover like he wanted everyone in Marietta to see him, would they?

But as he did just that, with the crisp fall afternoon gorgeous and gold around him and that snap in the breeze, it occurred to him that he had no experience when it came to chasing women. They'd always chased him. The naughtier ones had followed him around boldly when he'd been a boy, while the good ones had confined themselves to longing glances they'd thought he didn't notice. When he'd grown older and started making all that money, there'd been more women than he could count whenever he turned around. Wherever he went. At some point, the competition to get in his bed had slid into a fight to get his ring, and he understood, now, that he'd grown complacent with all that relentless attention. He hadn't been *nervous* about a female in as long as he could recall.

One more way Chelsea Collier was turning him inside out, he thought wryly. He supposed he'd just have to get used to it.

The parking lot was nearly empty when she finally appeared, and he thought his heart actually stopped in his chest at the sight of her.

She was so damned pretty. It snuck beneath his ribs and lodged somewhere underneath, like a stitch in his side, making it hard to concentrate on anything but the flirty swing of that dress around her lovely legs, the clever little buckles around her ankles that managed to be demure and sexy at once, and all of her gleaming blonde hair down around her shoulders today, so bright and something like joyful in the sunlight. She marched out of the double doors with a frown on her face, like she was leading a charge straight into some or other battle, and he knew the very moment she saw him there. Waiting for her.

It was satisfying in ways he couldn't articulate even to himself to see the hitch in her step, and then the way her walk changed, turned into more of a languid saunter, all hips and intent, like she could still feel him the way he still felt her. The way her pretty face smoothed out, and her lips twitched in the corners, inviting him to think some more on the stunning wickedness of that mouth of hers, all that carnal promise right there on her face for everyone to see.

How had the men in this place kept their hands off of her? *Idiots,* he thought.

"Have you been standing out here all afternoon?" she asked when she drew closer. He could see the sleepless night around her eyes, and thought it made her that much prettier. That much more *his.*

"Not *all* afternoon."

"You look like you've been here a while."

A delightful possibility occurred to him. "Are you trying to keep me your dirty secret? Oops. You should have made that clear, probably."

She eyed him for a moment, shifting the band of her bag higher on her shoulder.

"I think that specific cat leapt from that particular bag when I jumped on your motorcycle last night right there on Main Street in front of the entire town," she said, and then looked surprised when he laughed.

"I'm sorry." He wasn't, really, but she was the prettiest thing he'd ever seen and talking to her was the most exquisite torture he'd ever suffered. He wanted to be deep inside her again. He wanted to see if he'd ever conquer this craving for her that seemed to gnaw at him from deep in his own gut. "Do people really care what you do? Is this that whole small town thing? I thought that was a myth."

She smiled, and he loved it.

"The prevailing wisdom is that you're taking advantage of me, as a matter of fact," she said, leaning in closer as if imparting a deep, dark secret, and he could smell that almond scent on her hair. It made him hard, that easily. "What with your worldly, wealthy ways. I'm nothing but a small town girl, you know. Easily led astray."

"Am I the big, bad wolf in this scenario?"

"Of course." Her smile was very nearly wicked, and he wanted to lick it.

"Despite the fact that was you lounging around outside my house yesterday morning, tempting me to stray from the path of the righteousness? If anyone's the wolf, Triple C, it's you."

She liked the sound of that. He saw it in that flush of pleasure that moved over her, lighting up her eyes and her whole face, then down into the v-shaped neck of her dress. The dress he admired deeply and couldn't wait to peel right off that delicious body of hers.

"What about my virtue?" he asked lazily. "Why doesn't anyone care about that?"

"That's not how the story goes, I'm afraid," she told him with a happy sigh. "You don't get to change the role you've been assigned. Besides, I had the misfortune to date an idiot, and since I caught him cheating on me a few months ago, I *must* be broken hearted. That's the story, so that's the truth."

But she sounded amused by that, he noted.

"I caught my wife cheating on me," Jasper drawled. "Do

you know what I am?" He waited until her brows edged up. "Divorced."

Her eyes crinkled in the corners, and he thought he could watch that forever.

"I'll confess to you that I liked the *idea* of him more than I liked *him*," she went on, cheerfully. "And realizing I couldn't live with myself if I ignored the cheating was actually a bit of a relief. But that's not an interesting story. So, obviously, I must be acting out my feelings in inappropriate ways. That's where you come in." She shook her head. "Tempting me into letting my hair down. *Literally.*"

"I had no idea," he said, and then he couldn't take it anymore, he had to touch her. He reached over and took her hand, threading his fingers through hers. "I usually prefer to cause a commotion on purpose."

"You did that by moving here, especially into the Crawford Rail Depot, which everyone has heard my mother rant on and on about for years," she said, but she was staring at their linked fingers in a kind of wonder, and he didn't know what it was that clamored inside of him then, like church bells on a long Sunday morning. And he didn't care.

"FlintWorks Brewery," he corrected her, and grinned when she frowned at him. "That's what I'm calling it. But if you want, I can name a beer after you. Triple C has a nice ring to it. Or maybe Black Bart Ale?"

She kept frowning, and then she cleared her throat, and he went still like that was foreshadowing to an attack.

"I assumed last night was a one night stand," she said, matter-of-factly, and for once he couldn't read her expression even when she continued to stand there and hold his gaze so directly.

"I don't recall setting any restrictions."

"So… An affair, then?"

"Do we need a label?"

It didn't escape his notice that neither label she'd chosen suggested much in the way of longevity, but he only filed that away. For now.

"Sometimes," she said quietly, "labels can be helpful. They set out expectations ahead of time. They prevent confusion."

"If I plan to take advantage of you," he replied in the same tone, "I'll let you know, without any confusion at all. Like tonight, Chelsea, I plan to take extended advantage of you. Just as soon as I can get you naked. Do you need more than that?"

"People will talk," she said, her voice no more than a whisper, but he saw all the heat and fire and need from last night in her blue eyes, and he grinned.

"Sounds like they already are," he replied. "And there's no point letting all that speculation go to waste, is there?"

SEPTEMBER BLED INTO October, the town started showing signs of the rodeo, the wind started to smell of the coming change of seasons all the time, and Chelsea simply surrendered to the delicious madness. To all of it.

There was her mother's continued silence, which she couldn't do a thing about, so she simply ignored it. There were whispers behind certain hands when she walked into the faculty lounge at school or particular shops in town, but there were far more open smiles of approval and even the occasional thumbs up from others.

"Have you seen those pictures of his house?" Tricia Larssen asked in the checkout line of the supermarket. "I mean, his old house."

"He hasn't sat me down with any photo albums, if that's what you mean," Chelsea had said, not sure where this was going. Tricia was older than Chelsea by some fifteen years, and was known to prefer her dogs to most people.

"It had three indoor pools. A fifteen car garage. A sauna and its own bowling alley."

Chelsea had waited for the put down, the implication that she was too naïve or too small town to appreciate a man like Jasper. But Tricia Larssen had smiled.

"You go, girl," she said in her three-pack a day smoker's voice. "You go."

And the truth was, Chelsea didn't really have any time to analyze what was happening. Her life was always at a fever pitch this time of the year, and would have been crazy even without Jasper. There was school, Mama, and all the rodeo volunteer committees she always wished she hadn't agreed to take part in before signing right up again the minute it was over.

To say nothing of the final rush toward Jenny's big show of a wedding on Saturday, and all the events she was expected to be a part of leading up to it as Jenny's Maid of Honor. Maids of Honor didn't share their niggling concerns unless asked directly, she told herself sternly over and over again that week—and no one had asked her a thing.

So she kept her mouth shut and she lost herself in the wonder of Jasper's touch, his voice, his mouth on hers, his powerful body above her and below her, inside her, until she felt cracked wide open. Changed. New.

"Did you ever want to live somewhere else?" he asked that Friday. Jenny's rehearsal dinner had been earlier that night, and Chelsea had been unable to wait to slip away from the strange tension between bride and groom to be, unable to wait to run here, to Jasper, like he was some kind of homing beacon.

They were wrapped around each other in his bed now, and she could still hear his heart pounding in his chest below her ear. She smoothed her palm over it like she was trying to catch it, like fireflies in the summer.

"Of course," she said. "I wanted to live *anywhere* else. Madrid. Sydney. Bora-Bora. I used to sit in the travel section of the bookstore and lose myself in daydreams for hours. I wanted to see everything."

"What happened?"

His voice was that low rumble she loved more every time she heard it, and his fingers moved in her hair, toying with it like he couldn't get enough of touching her. Like he wanted her that much. As much as she wanted him.

"Every time I had the opportunity, I didn't want to go," she confessed. She waited for some negative reaction along the lines of the pitying looks her sister Margot always sent her way, the exasperated sighs her brother Nicky always let escape him when he came back home and saw all the things Chelsea still loved, like it was all beneath him now. "Maybe I was too afraid. Isn't that what keeps people close to home? Fear?"

His hand tightened on the back of her head, and he shifted, until she had no choice but to shift with him and look him in the face. Knowing how easily he could read her, she thought she'd never felt more naked than she did then.

"You don't strike me as afraid of much, Chelsea, or you wouldn't be here with me. Would you?"

She laughed, but it felt rusty, and she knew she should be worried about the heat she could feel pooling in the back of her eyes, making her feel glazed and precarious. Making her worry he was the only thing tethering her to the world.

"That's where you're wrong," she said, her voice so much more ragged than she'd wanted it to be, sharing too much. "I can't think of a single thing I'm not afraid of. I've been a coward all my life. I've hidden myself away here so I didn't have to face it. But that's the truth about me, Jasper. I'm sorry."

He looked at her for a long time, then he tucked her back against her shoulder, and it seemed like he rocked her a little bit, just slightly, like he was trying to soothe away the sting of her words.

But Chelsea knew better. She knew they burned in her, that if he looked close enough, the truth of them was all he'd see. The idea of that was unbearable.

"I've spent my whole life looking for a place worth hiding away in," he said after a while. "My daddy was a broken, bitter man. He used religion the way some men use alcohol, beating his form of humility into us. He used to pack my brother and me into his car and drive us on a tour of Dallas and all the things we'd never have. It took me years to realize it was what *he* couldn't have."

She leaned forward and pressed a kiss against the smooth skin of his shoulder.

"My brother Jonah and I decided we might as well show the old man the error of his ways." His voice was so cheerful. That lazy drawl and the suggestion that this was all just a colorful story, with no ominous currents beneath to tear into him. But she knew better, somehow. So she held him in the dark, like this golden, beautiful man was as damaged as she sometimes feared she was, and she listened. "So we did. We did whatever the hell we could to make money, and it turned out, we were good at it. I found myself a trophy wife, bought myself a house to match. I have planes, cars. Motorcycles. I've been everywhere, Chelsea. I've seen everything I ever wanted to see, and then some." He blew out a breath. "And about a year ago I was riding my bike through a part of the country I'd never seen before, and I stopped high up on a mountain road and looked out over this valley of yours, and I thought it looked perfect. It *felt* perfect." He wrote something incomprehensible against the smooth line of her spine, shapes and letters, hieroglyphs. "I decided I didn't want to be anywhere but here. So I don't know. Are you hiding? Or is this just where you belong?"

CHELSEA HELD ON to that the next day, when she stood in the cool church that stood haughtily in the best part of town, filled to the brim with all of Marietta's best and brightest. She held on to that hard as her all best friend's dreams came to a screeching halt when Charles Monmouth III called off the wedding and then left, like something out of a nightmare, leaving Jenny to stand up on that relic of an altar and announce, in a bloodless voice, that the wedding was off.

It was good to belong to a place like Marietta, she thought, where even Mama could set aside whatever petty snobberies she used to while away her days in the face of a real, honest-to-goodness crisis. Where the people who knew and loved Jenny simply took charge of things so she could quietly disappear after making her announcement, taking responsibility for making the calls and relaying the appropriate excuses.

Where no one questioned the fact that Jenny's Maid of Honor, who wished fervently she'd *said something,* had to sit by herself with her face in her hands for a little while, as if what had happened in that church had happened to her, too. Because everyone knew that she and Jenny had grown up in each other's pockets, and that Jenny's heartbreak meant Chelsea's, too.

She showed up at Jasper's while all the light was still pouring into the great windows that stood sentry all around his cavern of a loft, startling him. He started to speak but she shushed him, with her finger and then her mouth, hiking up the pastel Maid of Honor gown as she straddled him where he sat.

She didn't ask, she took. *She* took. She set the pace, she let her head drop down and she bit into his shoulder like some kind of untamed thing, and she forgot. She forgot about broken hearts, about shattered dreams. About the promises men made, about the terrible things people could do to each other. She rode him hard until all of that faded, loss and fear and the rest, until there was nothing left in the whole world but that wildfire, that slick burn, that magical place they made between them.

Until she made them both cry out as they hurtled over the edge, together.

It was a long time later that Jasper stirred beneath her, his hazel eyes wise and kind as he cupped her face in his hands, gazing much too intently into her face.

"Do you want to tell me what that was all about?"

She looked at him, and felt jagged. Ripped into too many pieces to ever put herself back together. Like what had happened to Jenny today was foreshadowing. Like there was nothing to stop her from careening straight into that very same wall, and breaking just the same.

"No," she said, and kissed him again, until he stopped asking questions that didn't have answers, and took her to his bed instead.

And for the first time in her life, Chelsea found she wished the rodeo wasn't coming to town that following week, because it meant that all the people she normally would have gone to for help or advice weren't available. Jenny wasn't an option, of course—but everyone else was too busy making sure Marietta was prepared for the influx of so many people, the participants as well as the audience, who would come from all over and expect the good old fashioned western rodeo the town had been putting on for seventy-five years. To say nothing of all the events surrounding it—the street dance and the parade, fundraising lunches and dinners, and the Saturday morning pancake breakfast that Crawfords had been flipping pancakes at every one of those seventy-five years.

"I'm so disappointed about the depot," Kira Blair, one of

the Crawford Railway Depot Museum's staunchest supporters, said when they saw each other on one of the roads outside of town that Monday, both stopping their cars to chat quickly before anyone else came along. "What was Tod thinking?"

"I've never been able to answer that question," Chelsea said with a grin, making the other woman laugh. "If I had, the last couple of years of my life would have been very, very different."

Kira looked as if she wanted to say something else, but one of the local ranchers drove up behind her in a big truck, and she only waved as she drove away.

So Chelsea pretended she was okay. Because she was okay, wasn't she? This was what adventurous looked like. This was how it felt. Outsized and obvious, but still—better than what had gone before. Better than her whole, previous life.

Better than what had happened on Saturday to Jenny, certainly, even if she knew she was on her own kind of borrowed time.

"I don't want to talk about the wedding," Jenny said tightly when they met each other on Tuesday outside Copper Mountain Chocolate on Main Street. She forced a smile. "I know *you* have a thousand things to tell me. Let's talk about that instead."

"Of course."

But Chelsea was more interested in taking Jenny inside

and making sure she picked out appropriately medicinal chocolate. Jenny looked small and lost and unlike herself, staring fiercely through the display case at a selection of truffles, and Chelsea had no idea what to do.

"How is she?" Sage Carrigan, the owner of the chocolate shop and a friend, asked in an undertone from behind the counter.

"I don't know," Chelsea said softly. "How *can* she be?"

Sage had been a bridesmaid too, and they shared a look then, like they were both reliving those awful moments inside the church. Jenny's brief disappearance and then her slow, horrible walk up the aisle in all that deafening silence, all in white and all alone.

"And what about you?" Sage asked, her dark look lightening as she looked from Jenny to Chelsea. "I've seen Jasper Flint. That man is hot."

"We have very interesting discussions, Sage," Chelsea said, pretending to be haughty. "I haven't really noticed."

Which made Jenny laugh, if only slightly, and that was what mattered. Not all the uncertain things that clamored inside of her, desperate to escape. This wasn't the time for her worries. She knew that.

"How's it going?" Jenny asked, and Chelsea wanted nothing more than to tell her. Everything. But that would be nothing but selfish. *This wasn't then time.*

"It's great," she said. "Absolutely *great*."

And then she smiled fiercely so neither Jenny nor Sage

could see how desperate she was to *talk* to someone, anyone. How desperate she was to have her friends dismiss her terrible fear that it was the finest joke in Montana history that *Chelsea Collier* thought she could attract the attention of a man like Jasper Flint. To hear them instead staunchly insist that *of course* she was that beautiful woman she thought she saw reflected in his eyes on those long, heated nights in his loft, that only idiots could possibly think otherwise—

Idiots like Tod, apparently.

"Chels," he said, coming up behind her while she was waiting for one of Mama's prescriptions—because the enduring Silent Treatment didn't mean Chelsea could forgo her usual chores and duties, it only meant they'd all be that much more unpleasant while she did them.

Chelsea started at the sound of his voice too close to her ear, dropping the cherry-flavored lip balm she'd been pretending to be so fascinated with while hiding out from Carol Bingley's censorious gaze.

Some people, it went without saying, were less supportive.

"How many times do I have to ask you to stop calling me that?" she mused aloud. She leaned down and scooped the tube of lip balm from the floor, then slapped it back on its shelf. "That's not a rhetorical question. I'm honestly curious. Do you not hear me when I ask you to stop or do you think I'm kidding? I can't figure it out."

He was frowning at her when she stopped talking, his

boyish looks not striking her as at all charming any longer. Not when she'd experienced what it was like to spend time with an actual, grown man. One who had yet to lie to her, about anything, because he claimed he liked her. A lot. It was astonishing how good that honesty made her feel, she realized then, no matter where this thing between them was or wasn't going. No matter how temporary it was.

"You're making a fool of yourself," Tod informed her. In that friendly way of his she no longer believed was particularly friendly at all.

She stared at him. "By picking up a prescription? How do you figure?"

"Don't play games with me."

"That's actually hilarious, coming from you."

"Listen," he said, magnanimously. "I know I was harsh with you the other day in the office. I know that must have hurt. I'm not proud of myself. You walked straight into this guy's clutches, and I get it, I do. This is my fault."

For the first time in months, Chelsea looked at Tod and realized she found him nothing but entertaining.

"I can't stand watching you do this to yourself," he said in the same ponderous tone, and she believed he meant that. The jerk.

"And by 'this,' you mean trading up?" she asked innocently.

Well. *Kind of* innocently.

"You're Chelsea Collier," he said flatly, once again voicing her fears. This time, she liked it even less. "You have a certain reputation in this town, and you know that. You can't start dressing like a barfly and hanging all over the first single man to look in your direction without people talking. What did you think would happen?"

"Oh," she said, aware she was adopting little bit of that lazy drawl Jasper used so well, but she couldn't seem to help herself. "You know. *Nothing*. Like what happened to you when I caught you with Leona."

"I knew you were still holding on to that."

He was less entertaining when she wanted to punch him, she found.

"I wouldn't say I was *holding on* so much as it's burned into my memory forever whether I like it or not, in a post-traumatic stress sort of way."

She pointed at herself, then swept her hand up and down, taking in what Tod apparently felt constituted a 'barfly' outfit. A pair of trousers she'd worn to work which, yes, fit her. And a long sleeved t-shirt that also fit her, not too tightly but not too loosely, either, beneath a pretty blue scarf. Hardly Mata Hari's first choice of vamping attire.

"But this? Is called shopping from my own closet." It was true; she hadn't bought a single new item of clothing. She'd simply stopped hiding herself away in the ones she had. "And the rest is called moving on. I would have thought you, of all people, would be thrilled."

"I care about you, Chelsea," Tod said, and though he

used that pompous tone, the fact he also actually used her name struck her as something of a victory. "I don't like to see you sink down to this level."

"I appreciate that," she said. And she tried to, she really did.

But it was the first time in memory that she'd been *relieved* to hear nosy Carol Bingley call her name.

She paid for Mama's pills and stood there pretending she didn't notice the way Carol was staring at her, until the other woman let out one of her trademark sniffs.

"Your poor mother," Carol said, her voice dripping with censure while Chelsea reminded herself that this was a lonely old woman, not a monster. That this was what sadness looked like unchecked. "To see the Crawford name come to this."

"Are the shades of Pemberley to be thus polluted?" Chelsea quoted theatrically, carrying on with the theme—and could see by Carol's frown that she was not up on her Jane Austen. Not a great surprise. Chelsea smiled instead, though it was starting to feel a lot more like a grimace. "My mother is fine, thank you. I'll tell her you said hello."

And still, she found herself knocking on Jasper's door as soon as she could make it back down into town after another painfully silent meal with her mother, and she left her car parked right there in front of the depot like the red flag it was, announcing her scandalous whereabouts to anyone who drove by.

"You look a little…" Jasper paused, standing in his open door in nothing but the kind of cargo pants that hung low on his narrow hips and still made it clear he was the richest man in town. "Intense."

"You look clothed," she retorted, and his hazel eyes went from that gleam of amusement to pure gold in a single hot instant.

"Easily remedied," he muttered, reaching out and yanking her inside.

And this was what mattered, she told herself as they succumbed to that wildness again, to the soaring fire and the shattering passion, right there on the other side of the door, up against his wall. These moments of the purest happiness were what she collected and what she'd hold close to her heart, like treasures, when all of this madness burned itself out.

Because she wasn't the naïve fool people idiots like Tod seemed to think. It didn't matter what Jasper had said about labels or restrictions. She hadn't had to look at those intrusive pictures of the house he'd owned in Dallas that were splashed all over the Internet—or the woman he'd shared it with and called his wife, trophy or not—to understand that they came from completely different worlds.

She knew that better than anyone. She was the one who tasted this man, lost herself in him, knew every last inch of his glorious body. She knew what it was to hold him and what it was to be held down by him. She knew that heart-breaking smile and she knew his roguish grin. That delicious drawl, still as thick and smooth as honey when he wanted it to be. That clever mouth, and that shrewd intelligence he hid behind his Texan routine. The way he could take her in his hands and make her mindlessly and entirely his, every time.

She knew.

This was the last, best stretch of fall in Montana. Rich golden days, endlessly clear nights, a last gasp of perfect weather before the bleak cold and endless dark ahead. Something to dream about when the snow started. Something to hold on to while the storms hurled themselves over the Rockies and reminded them why not everyone lived in a place like this, dreaming of the summers while winter did its worst. *She knew.*

Just like the poem said, better than she ever could:

Nothing gold could stay.

Chapter Eight

CHELSEA WAS EATING her usual school day breakfast of steel cut oats with a dash of milk and honey, staring out the windows of the breakfast nook off the kitchen that Mama liked to call her *morning room,* not seeing the tall pines or the town clustered along the river below or the white-tipped mountains in the distance. She was thinking about Jasper, lost in a cascade of extremely carnal images from the night before. His deep, hot kiss when she'd knocked on his door, his hands fisted in her hair. The way she'd knelt before him. The look in his eyes when she'd taken him deep in her mouth—

Mama, who had been maintaining her affronted, chilly silence for more than a week, even through the wedding and its aftermath, cleared her throat. Pointedly. Making Chelsea jump and flush hot, as if she'd been broadcasting the images in her head all over the kitchen wall.

"The rodeo is coming to town," Mama observed from her usual place at the table, the paper opened before her, though her eyes were on Chelsea. "The streets will be filled with all the usual carrying on. Bad decisions and public embarrassments from here to Bozeman, just like every other year." She stared at Chelsea, who had gone still in her seat, her oatmeal forgotten. "But then everything will get back to normal. You'll still be a rural schoolteacher with a quiet little life. And *he'll* still be a billionaire and the man responsible for destroying this family's legacy. What then, Chelsea?"

"What do you mean, what then?" Her voice was light, thank goodness. Not as wary as she felt. Not tinged with the darkness of all the things she feared. "What do you think is going to happen?"

"I think he's going to smash your heart into pieces, shame you and this family even more than he already has, and then disappear."

Her mother's voice wasn't cold then, or furious—both of which Chelsea could have handled. Instead, it was soft. Something like wistful. And impossibly, unutterably sad.

"Mama," Chelsea murmured, trying hard to be gentle, to keep her tone respectful. To keep her confusion and panic at bay. "You don't even know him."

"You think I'm an old, silly fool," her mother said then. "And I won't pretend I don't give you cause. But you're not the first girl in the world to have your head turned by the wrong man, Chelsea. Look at what happened to that friend of yours. Men come and go. They mean what they say when they whisper it in your ear, but then something else comes along and it turns out they mean that, too. Usually more."

She lifted her hands, encompassing the sunny kitchen they sat in. The house. The view of Chelsea's whole world right there outside the windows, like a finely-rendered painting she could see in all its perfect detail even with her eyes closed. "This is what matters. This is what endures. Your family name. Your history. Your place in the march of time, no matter what you did with your individual days. No matter what they whispered about you."

She wasn't talking about Chelsea, or even Jenny's wedding. It came like a flash, that understanding, and it was profoundly dislocating. It was easier to think of her mother as a cantankerous old character she had to work around, to placate, to care for. It was something else entirely to think of her as a person in her own right, possessed of her own, complicated history. And perhaps far lonelier than Chelsea had imagined.

It wasn't an understanding she particularly wanted, Chelsea realized, and that made her deeply ashamed of herself.

"You've made your mark here," she said after a moment. "Whether there's ever a Crawford Museum or not, *you* have been a tireless volunteer for every single cause I can think of, Mama. The library, the school board, the new hospital. Isn't that enough of a legacy?"

"I understand my place," Mama said after another long moment, and it felt to Chelsea like there were too many things unsaid in the air between them, thick like smoke and far more treacherous. "Oh, I dreamed of other things, other places. Who doesn't? I wanted to go to Ireland and live a while in all that green. I wanted to be a dancer."

"I didn't know you danced," Chelsea said, absurdly charmed at the notion.

"I don't," Mama replied evenly. "And I've never been to Ireland, either."

She reached over and slid a hand over Chelsea's, and when Chelsea looked down, it was like looking at some kind of time-lapse photograph. Her mother's knuckles were a bit larger, thanks to the Crawford family curse of arthritis, and the veins more pronounced, but their hands were the same. The same narrow fingers, the same shaped backs of their palms. The same size, even.

"You're kinder than I've ever been," Mama said in a low voice. "Smarter, too, and I would have killed for that hair when I was young. But beneath that, we're the same, Chelsea. You're meant for this place, this town. Your brother and your sister were restless spirits, always looking for whatever lay on the other side of the horizon, but not you."

"Mama…" She didn't know what she meant to say, but there was a great pressure on her chest then, like a band tightening around her ribs, and she knew only that she didn't want to hear this. Whatever it was.

But her mother didn't stop. "When they looked up at the stars, you were sinking your feet deep in the ground where you stood. From the time you were a baby."

"I don't know what that means," Chelsea whispered,

stricken.

"Yes," Mama said, matter-of-factly. She squeezed Chelsea's hand once, hard. "You do."

SHE FOUND HIM in the lower level of the depot late that afternoon, after she'd finished with another day of teaching and then a good hour or so of sitting in her classroom, putting off the inevitable. Chelsea walked inside, taking a moment to appreciate the graceful old lines of the building, the little flourishes that whispered of the lost Old West, and the light still streaming in from outside.

She wanted to do anything but this.

Jasper had his cellphone clamped to his ear while he leaned over a drafting table in the far corner of the great room, making notes on the blueprints he'd showed her before. He was talking about his taproom and tasting room, his brewing tanks and the complicated state laws that governed beer production, and Chelsea tuned out the words as she stood there.

It was that voice of his she loved, that deep, raspy drawl. It was the hard perfection of his very male form, packed into jeans and a tight-fitting Henley, that made her mouth water involuntarily. It was the way he shoved his hand into his hair and raked it back, and that sexy crook of his mouth when he looked up and saw her standing there.

"I didn't expect you until later," he said when he finished

his call, tossing his phone carelessly on to the table.

She wanted to stand there forever. She wanted to soak him in, drown in him, until she couldn't tell the difference between the two of them any longer. The way she felt when he drove her to that edge and held her there, before hurling them both over the side and into oblivion. She wanted to stay right here, right now, right in this moment, like nothing else existed or ever could.

But Mama had been right. No matter how Chelsea had tried to rationalize it away. Mama might be a snob. She might have been huffy and quick to take offense. She might even have caused more than her share of trouble, because she'd always been a character. But that didn't make her wrong about Chelsea.

Roots and history. Marietta down into her bones. That was who Chelsea was, who she'd *chosen* to be. That was who she'd stay. She'd become her mother because she was already like her mother, and maybe, deep inside, she'd always known that. Maybe that was why no matter how hard she'd dreamed and plotted and pretended, she'd never tried very hard to get away from Marietta. Maybe this was her own little half-hearted rebellion about the inevitable.

But if Jenny's wedding had taught her anything, it was that she *liked* the inevitable. She liked her small town. She liked all the characters she shared it with. She liked being part of their story. That wasn't going to change. She wasn't going to leave.

And Jasper Flint was like those stars her brother and sister had hungered for throughout their youth, a brilliant mess of light against the dark Montana skies, and much too far away no matter how close he seemed. Never hers. Not really.

She wasn't sure he knew that, but she did. And she also knew that she'd fallen heedlessly and foolishly in love with this man, practically from the first moment she'd set eyes on him. If she didn't walk away now, she never would.

Mama was right about that, too: he'd crush her when he left.

And Chelsea had no doubt that he'd leave. He wouldn't be able to help himself. That was what men like him did. Like Charles Monmouth had done on his wedding day to Jenny, like winter followed fall. It was who Jasper was. She could no more begrudge that than she could damn the stars above her head for their shine.

But he was walking toward her in that same low, confident way he'd done the morning they'd met, and she knew that if she let him touch her, she'd lose the will to do this. And she had to do this.

"I'm not coming later," she said, blurting it out before she could convince herself not to do it, to wait, to think, to put it off a while longer. "I only came now to say goodbye."

He stopped walking all of two strides away, and then went still.

Too still.

"Are you going on a trip?" His tone was too even, too

polite. She knew better than to believe it.

"This can't work," she said, screwing up her courage and tipping her chin back as she threw it out there. "We both know that. I think it's time we ended it, before anyone gets hurt."

"I think someone always gets hurt, Triple C. That's the game."

"I don't want to play games." She cleared her throat, tried not to melt at that look in his eyes. "I don't want to play at all."

"What's this about?" he asked softly, and she wanted nothing more than to close the distance between them, melt into him, let him hold her. But she couldn't let that happen. She didn't want to lose herself any more than she already had. "The gossip?"

"I don't care about gossip," she bit out, holding herself tight and still, like she didn't know what she'd do if she eased up on her own grip.

"Of course you do," he contradicted her. "You live here."

She supposed she shouldn't be surprised they'd come such a long way in so short a time, that the two of them should switch positions like that. But then again, if they hadn't come so far, this wouldn't hurt.

She couldn't let herself think about how much it hurt.

"I'll come and have a beer in the spring," she told him. "When you open."

"Is that supposed to be my consolation prize?" His drawl

was more pronounced, his eyes narrowed and bright with temper, and he crossed his arms over his chest. "Lucky me."

"Please don't make this hard."

"Did you think I'd take it well?" He laughed, short and unhappy. "I spent most of last night so deep inside you I forgot my name. I know how you taste. I'm not okay with this, Chelsea."

"You don't have to be okay with it," she said quickly, ignoring the images he'd thrown into her head. Ignoring her body's reaction to it, to him, like clockwork. "Though I suspect you're just unused to someone else making a decision for you." She smiled at him then, and making that smile look real was one of the hardest things she'd ever done, but she managed it. "You don't want me, Jasper. When the novelty wears off, you won't remember why you ever did."

That hurt her more to say than it could possibly have hurt him, despite the way he flinched, like she'd hit him. Chelsea turned around and started for the door, determined to get away from him. It was done, and that was what mattered. The pain was something she'd just have to figure out how to survive—

But his hands were on her, suddenly, turning her back around to face him, and then his mouth slammed over hers.

That damned fire.

That wild, impossible need.

It roared through her, scalding her. Making her shiver and burn. Making her melt into him the way she always did, meeting each hard kiss, each claiming stroke of his tongue. She couldn't resist him. She didn't *want* to resist him—

But that was all the more reason she had to leave him.

It actually caused her physical pain to wrench herself away from him.

"This is bullshit."

His voice was harsh. Succinct. And Chelsea couldn't seem to do anything but stare at him.

He was still holding her shoulders in his hands, and he was so close to her, that beautiful face of his *so close* and those bright hazel eyes of his searching every part of her, tearing her asunder, shining a light where there had never been anything but shadow.

"You don't have to hide anymore," he told her, his voice low and determined. "You don't—"

"Jasper." Even his name hurt. Misery almost knocked her from her feet to her knees, but she stepped back, away from him, and somehow she didn't fall. "This is temporary. This has never been anything but temporary, and I have to go. You have to let me."

"I don't want to." Fierce and sure, and was that pain in his gaze? Thick and sharp at once? She didn't understand that. She couldn't let herself look any closer. "I don't understand this."

"You will," she said, not letting herself waver. Not letting herself reach out to him the way she wanted to do, so much that her fingers ached with need of him. "Sooner than you think, I'd imagine."

And then, finally, she turned and ran.

JASPER STOOD IN the howling emptiness she left behind her for a long time, thinking about the word *temporary*.

He'd made it the cornerstone of his life. Growing up, he and his brother had vowed they'd get the hell away from their father at the first available opportunity, so they'd never let themselves get too attached to any of the places or people they encountered while under his mean, violent thumb. When they'd built the business, they'd been solely focused on money. Becoming solvent. Then becoming rich. Then making sure they'd be very, very wealthy for the rest of their lives no matter what they did.

But each step in that process, Jasper had known it was temporary. He'd known that damned house in Dallas wasn't permanent. He'd always envisioned himself somewhere else, which was why he hadn't much cared what Marlene and her decorator did with the place. He hadn't really thought about it in those terms, but he supposed that he'd always thought Marlene was temporary too. God knew, when he'd announced he was selling the company and leaving the oil business entirely, he hadn't expected her to come along with him on whatever his next adventure was.

What exactly are you planning to do with your retirement? she'd asked, not pausing in the series of crunches she was performing in their home gym. He'd always admired Marlene's commitment to what, he supposed in retrospect, was *her* business: that flawless body of hers. She'd sounded mildly curious, at best, and not in the least bit winded.

Jasper had shrugged. *I don't know. Sell everything. Wander.*

Marlene had paused then, meeting his gaze from across the room, hers very cool. Very direct.

Do you expect me to accompany you on this journey into the life of a vagabond?

And he'd laughed. He'd never imagined that, he was certain she'd never imagined it, and he hadn't been particularly surprised when he'd found her in bed with her personal trainer shortly thereafter. Not pleased, certainly, but not surprised.

Temporary.

He didn't know how long he stood there in the very beginnings of what would be his microbrewery, but the shadows were long when he finally shook himself out of his daze. He found himself outside, walking down Main Street as the sun dropped toward the far hills and the colder air swept in.

Marietta sparkled in the last of the day's golden light. Banners welcoming the rodeo this coming weekend hung in all the shop windows, and there were lights strung up from lamppost to lamppost, creating a canopy of twinkling lights down the length of Main Street. He'd lived in this place all of a week and a half, and yet at least three people said hello to him as he passed. A very friendly shopkeeper. The rancher he'd met at the coffee shop one morning, who'd engaged him in a lively discussion about construction while they waited in line to get breakfast. The older woman who worked in his realtor's office, who'd brought him a welcome basket his first night in town.

He paused for a moment on the corner and let it settle in on him, the fact that he lived here now. That he really lived here. That unlike in Dallas, where he'd lived behind electronic gates and didn't know the names of his own staff, people expected to know him here. They greeted him, even when he had the kind of look on his face that could only be described as forbidding. This little jewel of a village he'd glimpsed from far off, that had looked exactly like the fantasy of home he'd carried around in his head all these years without knowing it, was home.

He was home, at last.

And nothing about what he felt about this place—much less about Chelsea—was *temporary.*

He found himself in the saloon, pulling up to a seat at the bar, not surprised to feel Jason Grey's brooding gaze on him, as unfriendly as ever. But it was the other, younger man Chelsea had called Reese who slid him a shot of whiskey, and smiled slightly when Jasper looked at him.

"Look like you need it," was all he said.

"I believe I do," Jasper agreed, and knocked it back.

He had no intention of letting her go. But he understood the value of a strategic retreat. He hadn't been a major player in a cutthroat business by accident.

"That look on your face says *woman trouble*," the bartender said, polishing a glass and setting it down. "But I know that's impossible."

Jasper only eyed him for a moment. Waiting.

"Everyone around here likes Chelsea." Reese nodded toward the other end of the bar, where Jason Grey stood, glowering. "Especially Jason, and he doesn't like anybody."

"Luckily," Jasper drawled, nodding when Reese moved to refill his glass, "I do, too."

The other man jerked his chin as if they'd solved a major problem, and then moved off down the bar toward a group of newcomers. It occurred to Jasper, belatedly, that he'd just been quizzed on his intentions. And he thought he understood, in a way he hadn't before, what it meant to have the kind of roots Chelsea did. To be seen and supported by all of these people, because they'd known her all her life. Because they were all a part of that life. It was all part and parcel of something bigger.

And that was why, the following morning, he drove up the mountain to Black Bart Road once he was sure school was in session, then took that winding drive up toward the house. He hadn't seen it in daylight before, and it was even prettier than it looked in the dark. It was a Victorian masterpiece, all gables and bay windows, rambling all over the hilltop it commanded in rich, dark colors, a piece of fairytale whimsy surrounded by rugged Montana splendor on all sides.

History wasn't just her job, he understood now, standing before this house Chelsea's ancestors had made with their hands. It made her who she was. It *was* who she was.

So he walked up to the door and knocked, because he had plans for that history. And her future, too.

Chapter Nine

"CAN I HAVE your attention, please?"

Chelsea froze at the sound of that voice—that deep drawl, entirely too delicious even broadcast over the speakers that projected him all the way down Main Street. She fought the urge to turn and stare at the makeshift stage where, until a second ago, the rowdy local band had been playing.

Of course, that only meant that she saw the way every single person in her line of sight turned to look at *her*. Most of them with giant grins on their faces.

She had no idea what Jasper was doing. She hadn't seen him since that unpleasant final scene in the depot, and she *certainly was not* replaying that last kiss over and over and over in her head. Just as she *absolutely hadn't* deliberately come to the street dance on Main Street—one of the kick off events of the rodeo, and also one of the events she'd helped put on—late enough to blend into the crowd.

Chelsea had no idea how Jasper felt about dances, but she'd told herself that on the off chance he didn't avoid this one altogether, she'd do better to be as inconspicuous as possible.

"I'm Jasper Flint," he was saying in that way of his, that snuck inside of her and turned everything bright and smooth. "As many of you know, I'm planning to turn the old railway depot into a microbrewery. We're planning to open in the spring, should I survive my first Montana winter."

Everyone laughed, of course, because there were a lot of enthusiastic folks around in the fall who left, thin-lipped and beaten down, come the far-off spring. Montana wasn't for everyone. Chelsea might have laughed herself, if it hadn't been so extraordinarily painful to hear his voice. She shifted slightly so she could see him, and that was worse. Much worse.

He was even more beautiful than usual tonight, dressed like a cowboy, in a hat and boots that felt like a little bit of sunshine on her country girl soul. This far away, she couldn't see the gleam in his eyes, but she recognized that smile of his, crooked and perfect.

It had been two days without him and it felt like years.

She had, she thought then, perhaps overestimated her ability to handle seeing him, even in public.

"But I don't want my arrival in Marietta, which I plan to make my home for a long time to come, to be marked by what I know some might see as a disrespect for its long history."

There was all that warmth in his voice. That hint of laughter, and Chelsea was so busy concentrating on how much she didn't want to react to him that it took her long moments to make sense of the figure who appeared up there next to him on stage. Because it didn't make any sense.

"It's my great pleasure to announce that in addition to renovating the railway depot, I'll be turning the historic Crawford House into a partial museum, which will help bring the story of this town and its people to a broader audience. I look forward to the challenge of living up to this town's history."

Mama was right there next to him while Jasper said this, smiling broadly as she applauded, and Chelsea still couldn't quite make sense of it. Of any of it. The people around her congratulated her, and more of the town seemed pleased by this announcement than Tod's comments on the First Families might have led her to believe, but even so, she couldn't seem to find her footing.

"So without further ado, I'll let y'all get back to this fine dance and this rodeo weekend," he said, and nodded at the band, who launched into a new song. "I look forward to many more, right here in Marietta."

Chelsea took that as her cue to bolt, and turned away, heading for her car. For escape. For space and clarity, to think through what had just happened, what Jasper and her mother must have planned, together, behind her back—

"Chelsea Crawford Collier." Still on all those speakers.

Loud and impossible to ignore, her name like a shout straight down the center of town. "Are you going to dance with me or not?"

She would have chosen *not*.

But all her friends and neighbors were laughing and clapping as if this was a happy scene out of some movie, and then they all stepped aside, opening up an aisle that led directly to her. And Jasper jumped down from the stage and prowled his way down it, that light in his eyes that made her pulse thump hard and then go wild.

She wanted to run. But she couldn't, not with everyone watching, because she didn't know if she'd run away from him—or straight to him.

And he knew it. She could see it in his swagger.

"What if I don't want to dance with you?" she asked when he was near.

"You do."

He grinned at her, a crook of those perfect lips, and then he swept her into his arms without waiting for her to respond, and suddenly there was nothing but fire.

All of that glorious fire.

It arced from his hand to hers. It was there between them when he pulled her closer to his chest, pulling her hard against him, making her wonder what her subconscious had been up to when she'd dressed tonight, in a dress she never wore that showed more of her curves than usual and the bright red cowboy boots she only pulled out for the rodeo.

Had she dressed for him, all the while telling herself she wasn't doing anything of the kind?

She felt his hand smooth down her back, heard his small, fervent sigh in her ear, and she knew she had.

Of course she had.

"Did you get all that?" He sounded amused, the way he almost always did, his mouth at her ear. "That's two long term projects, one of which involves close contact with your mother. I'm sending you a message. I'm not going anywhere."

"Jasper—"

He stopped moving then, and angled away from her, forcing her to tilt her head back to look up at him. His face had gone very serious, and it made her breath catch and her heart hurt.

"Of course it's scary," he said. "Do you think I'm not scared, too? But that's the *point*. That's what this is all about."

She didn't pretend she didn't understand him.

"I just think it will hurt less now," she said, with more determination than conviction.

"How's that working out?" he retorted, and there was something in his gaze then, kind and demanding at once, that made everything inside of her twist. Hard.

Because the truth was, it wasn't working out at all.

"What if you change your mind?" she asked, her voice so much stronger than she felt. "What if tomorrow you wake up and decide you have to visit Mozambique, immediately? What will you do then?"

His mouth crooked. "Ask you if you have a passport. Get you one if you don't."

And Chelsea couldn't help herself. She smiled.

He moved closer, sliding his hands around her to rest on her waist, pulling her in closer than was strictly appropriate in the middle of all these people, but Chelsea couldn't bring herself to care.

"It's crazy," he said, "but this felt like forever the moment I met you."

Chelsea tipped her head back, dizzy from the lights strung above him and the wild, sweet light in his beautiful eyes. From the stars above and from him, and she stopped fighting. It was time to live. Like he said, that was the whole point, no matter what happened.

"That sounds a little bit like *I love you,*" she pointed out.

His eyes gleamed brighter, and she understood, at last, that it was possible to spin around in all the stars in the dark sky without ever losing touch with the earth beneath her feet.

"It really does," Jasper agreed. "But I think that kind of thing needs time. To grow. To be sure. Months and months of time, Triple C. Maybe even years."

She looped her arms around his neck, loving that look on his face, loving him. Loving whatever came next, as long as it came with him.

"Let's find out," she said.

But first, they danced.

Around and around on Marietta's pretty Main Street, surrounded by all of those smiling friends and neighbors who cared how it ended, with the fall night like a blessing dressed up in giddy music, and the promise of forever in both of their smiles.

The End

If you enjoyed **Tempt Me, Cowboy**, you will love these other Montana Born stories by Megan Crane!

A Game of Brides
Please Me, Cowboy
Come Home for Christmas, Cowboy
In Bed with the Bachelor

Bad Boy Short Story
Project Virgin

Single Titles
I Love the 80s
Once More with Feeling

Available now at your favorite online retailer!

About the Author

USA Today bestselling, RITA-nominated, and critically-acclaimed author **Megan Crane** has written more than fifty books since her debut in 2004. She has been published by a variety of publishers, including each of New York's Big Five. She's won fans with her women's fiction, chick lit, and work-for-hire young adult novels as well as with the Harlequin Presents she writes as **Caitlin Crews**. These days her focus is on contemporary romance from small town to international glamor, cowboys to bikers, and beyond. She sometimes teaches creative writing classes both online at mediabistro.com and at UCLA Extension's prestigious Writers' Program, where she finally utilizes the MA and PhD in English Literature she received from the University of York in York, England. She currently lives in the Pacific Northwest with a husband who draws comics and animation storyboards and their menagerie of ridiculous animals.

For more info, visit Megan at www.MeganCrane.com.

Thank you for reading

Tempt Me, Cowboy

If you enjoyed this book, you can find more from all our great authors at TulePublishing.com, or from your favorite online retailer.

Made in United States
Troutdale, OR
11/01/2024

24345645R00080